For Dad

Welcome!

Congratulations on your first steps to get back into reading. You will thank yourself for it, I promise.

Many of us who love reading never pick up a book. Why not? I couldn't understand it until it happened to me. For me, I stopped either just after I had one of my babies or when I was grieving.

Two vastly different life events, but the result was the same. I was:

- Overwhelmed with new emotions
- Struggling with concentration
- Sleep deprived
- Living day by day

Unconsciously, I stopped reading, and I hated it. I truly believe if I had spent a few minutes a day reading, I would have felt better. Modern life is stressful, and we often put our wellbeing last. We don't have time, we are exhausted, and our heads are full of a million things already!

Every time I stopped reading, I trained myself back into it in the same way – with short stories. Every day, I felt a small success and I celebrated it. It couldn't be simpler! For the next 28 days, read one story a day. They start at less than 100 words (that's less than a minute you need to find!). The stories are all different and designed to ignite your imagination and open your mind, but most of all to make you fall in love with reading, so it finds its place in your life again.

Week One

Let's get started!

Take it one day at a time. You know your life and what works best for you. The stories for days 1-7 are all under 500 words, so you need to find less than five minutes each day. Be sure to celebrate your success at the end of the week.

Enjoy!

Day 1

No Escape

I'm behind the locked door but I am not safe. They know I am here and will come for me any minute. I can't cope and I weep silently, huddled on the floor. I've nothing left, they've taken everything. I hear the chaos and the war continuing and push my fingers deep into my ears. I hear the thunderous banging, but it's too late, they are outside.

"Mum!"

I sigh and splash my face. "One second please, kids, I'm just on the loo."

Day 2

My First Time

I wait nervously in the bedroom. He will be my first; what if I do it wrong? I have read about it, but that's not the same as doing it. My palms are sweaty, and I am shaking all over. He climbs onto the bed, it's dark but I can feel the weight of him above me. It's now or never and I know it's what I want.

I thrust the fire poker up through the mattress and into his body. He thrashes around and then is still. That was easy. I don't know what I was worried about. Now, on to the next job.

Day 3

See With Your Eyes

I sink onto the sofa with a cup of tea. Toddlers are exhausting, time to relax. Maisie seems happy playing on the floor.

"The king was in the counting house, counting out his money..." she sings while counting money from her toy purse.

"That's a lovely song Maisie." I clap, and she beams.

"I know, Mama, the boy and girl who live under your bed taught it to me." I feel my skin prickle and my blood runs ice cold. I struggle to speak.

"Maisie, don't be..."

"I don't know how they count without their eyes though."

My mouth dries and I spill tea onto my hands. Maisie jumps up and skips towards me.

"Can we all go and play?"

Day 4

Alive

Life always goes on, but often I think it shouldn't. I see hundreds of people every day, walking around like nothing's happened, like nothing has changed. I don't know how the world still turns. I want to scream at them all. Can't they see?

I serve my next customer. "Same again, love?"

"Yes, please, sweetheart."

I smile easily. My cracks are covered by the mask I paint on my face to look and feel like a person. Underneath, I'm not a real person anymore, maybe a shadow or a suggestion of a person.

My phone beeps. It's a text from Sarah. "Just at yours with Jackson, c u soon x."

I think I love my daughter and my grandson but I'm not sure I feel anything properly anymore. It's like the sound got turned down and I just have to wade through it. I know I'm still something, I just don't think I'm alive. I died when she did.

Day 5

Lose Control

When she jumps in the front seat of my cab, her legs get tangled in her huge, overflowing bag and stack of paper folders. I can feel the heat radiating from her. I know she won't acknowledge me; she would rather I just drive. Her eyes are fierce, and she is yelling down her phone, her other hand balled tightly into a fist.

"It doesn't matter, I'm on my way now. I look shit at my job for the millionth time, it's your only day to do it, Steve, why is your job more..."

He hangs up, and I watch it happen. Her eyes fill, she drops her phone and screams. The scream is pure pain and misery. She turns and grabs my wheel, pulling it violently towards her in an agonising release, and we screech to a stop.

"I'm so..." She is horrified and surprised by her actions and doesn't realise she couldn't stop herself. I watch her stumble out, gathering and spilling her belongings onto the wet ground. I wrap my fingers around it in my pocket and get out of the car. I crouch down and show her my police badge.

"I'm so sorry, I've never..."

I hold my hands up and interrupt her. "I used to be, until I lost control one day."

"Oh, I'm sorry. I'm so sorry for doing that, it's not like me at all."

"That's the point, it's not like you until one day it is, and by then it's too late."

She nods. "OK, thank you, I'll just get my... sorry again."

She is not ready to listen, but I have to try, I can see the frayed edges, I can sense the familiar impending crash.

"Be kind to yourself, take some time, you cannot control the depth of the emotion you feel or..."

"OK, bye, I have to go, I need to be somewhere."

I have to just watch her leave. You can't help everyone.

Day 6

Take A Chance

I'm bored. I sip my coffee and tap away on my laptop. She catches me staring and is not amused. I pretend to look at a table of attractive men in sharp suits behind her, but she doesn't buy it. I know I'm in trouble, but I'm mesmerised by her beautiful black hair and her hips swishing towards me.

She grabs the front of my shirt with both hands and lifts me up. "Listen to me!"

"Whoa, hold on a..."

Before I can say another word, we are on the ground.

"Stay down!" She presses her body against me. I am deafened by shouts and bangs and suddenly there are police and guns everywhere. She is still on top of me while the police round up the table of men in suits. My mates will be so jealous.

"I'm Maro," I whisper. "This is really cool."

"You could have been shot! You still could be! How can you say this is cool? It's not a movie!"

I'm not listening. Her eyes are dark and absorbing.

"It's a lot like a movie though. Are you a cop?"

"Can you be quiet, please? You're putting us both in danger."

"Sorry... are you a spy? Is this like a drug bust?"

She glares and puts her finger to her lips to shush me. "Are you five?"

"Shit, sorry, it's just…"

"I'll shoot you myself if I have to."

I think she likes me. "Do you have a gun? Can I see it? Not now obviously. We could meet later?"

She ignores me and I try to distract myself from her weight pressing down on my body. Suddenly she jumps up.

"You have to go and talk to that police officer over there before you can leave."

Disappointingly, her colleague looks more hobbit than man. "I'd rather talk to you instead?"

"No chance, that was like guarding an oversized toddler." She turns and swishes away. I can't wait to tell my friends.

Day 7

Special Delivery

"Delivery, can you sign here, please?" It's the fourth time this week and probably the hundredth time I've been here, and I don't think she has acknowledged me more than a handful of times. I hand her the screen and she scrawls on it. There is a kid about two years old pulling at her sleeve and she is ignoring her, too.

"Mummy, Henry put my toothbrush in his mouth." I can hear the two other children inside the house: spoiled brats. I don't know why she had them. The house is worth ten times the price of my flat. Why does she have to order so many things? She can because she has money, and she doesn't care about me.

I am back two days later.

"Delivery for you." There's a weird pause and she holds out her hand. Her face is flushed, her eyes are wandering and confused.

"No signature today." She grabs the package, rolls her eyes, and shakes her head before closing the door. She thinks she's special, she thinks I am nothing.

It's the third time this week. I park down the street and open today's package. It's two skirts that cost more than I earn in a week. She doesn't appreciate anything. With great satisfaction, I rub them on the floor and tape the package back up.

"Package for Mr Lindberg?"

"Actually, I think it's for me, Mrs Lindberg?" She is friendly today; I don't hear the children and she has a large glass of wine in her hand.

"Anyway, he doesn't..." She stops herself, "...order much. Not like me." She laughs nervously and I smile. "See you in a few days!" More nervous laughter. I finish my route. One ungrateful and overindulgent creature after another; the whole world is turning rotten.

I've waited all day for my delivery. He's usually so punctual, so I hope something hasn't happened to him. I really need my new handbag before the weekend. He's a bit of a sad case so I'd be quite pleased if he's been replaced. I almost let it slip yesterday that I live alone. I'll complain in the morning.

I never get a full night's sleep. One of the kids always wakes me up shouting, or trying to sleep in my bed. The door opens a crack. I think it's Agnes.

"What's up, sweetheart?"

"I had a bad dream."

I'm tired and can't be bothered to fight it. "Come around and jump in beside me."

"I won't fit in between you and Daddy."

"You know Daddy doesn't live..."

I feel a hand on my shoulder and his breath in my ear. "Delivery for you."

Week Two

Congratulations on completing Week One!

I hope you've enjoyed the stories so far. They aren't designed to be difficult or complicated, they are intended to be enjoyed and to stimulate different parts of your imagination and emotions.

The stories in Week Two are all between 500 and 1000 words, and you should find you need less than 10 minutes a day. Keep at it and by the end of Week Two it will start to feel like part of your daily routine.

Remember to celebrate your achievements!

Day 8

Food for Thought

We make brief eye contact for the third time. He is beautiful, with a warm, sexy smile and he can't take his eyes off me. What could be more wonderful than love at first sight on a train? I stare out of the window, looking thoughtful and mysterious. I run my ring-free left hand slowly through my hair.

"Tickets please, love." The conductor's protruding belly is closer to me than I would like. I find my ticket and sneak a look to see if he is watching. His piercing eyes are fixed on me; he is brushing his fingers across his gorgeous lips and smiling. I can barely contain my excitement. I've been waiting for this my whole life. The fat conductor smells like onions and I wish he would leave so I can continue my love story. I look up at him impatiently.

"You've got something on your face, love." He reaches his big hairy paw out towards me. I am horrified and lean away before his chubby fingers touch me.

"I'll sort it, thanks." I bat him away and hide to check my face on my phone. I could die. There is a disgusting blob of cream cheese on my upper lip. I'm not coming out from here, ever. Prince Charming doesn't want to kiss me at all, he just wants me to sort out my food-infested face. There's ten minutes until the next stop where I can get off and die of embarrassment. I peer through the seats; he is still looking at me and he is laughing!

How dare he? I have the worst taste in men. How could I have been so wrong about him?

Ten minutes feels like ten hours. I can't resist a peek through the seats at him every couple of minutes, but he's not looking anymore, he's reading a book. I knew he would be smart as well as draw-droppingly handsome. This is so unfair.

The train pulls in, and it's the last stop. I dash to the door behind me, almost taking out an old lady with a shopping cart. Completely pointless, as the platform is insanely busy and the old lady I pushed past shakes her fist at me. I don't need this shit. There's no way through and I have to go with the crowd. I can't face him laughing at me again.

I feel a gentle tap on my shoulder. He is even more beautiful up close. Gently, he puts his hand to my lips.

"You are easily the most beautiful woman I have ever seen with cheese on her face." I flush, he laughs. "Too soon?"

"You laughed at me, and I thought we..." He puts both hands firmly on my shoulders and stares deep into my eyes.

"I laughed because it was funny." He kisses me softly and everything melts away. We stand still and the crowd starts to dissipate around us. He takes my hand and we leave the station together. The rest of the world seems to vanish, nothing else matters and I know that this is the start of something amazing.

Day 9

Home Sweet Home

We are in the house we have always dreamed of: classic Victorian with fireplaces in every room and beautiful bay windows where I will sit and read. Don't get me wrong, it's been a difficult road, but we made it, we survived it all. We sit on boxes in our new living room and devour well-deserved fish and chips.

"Have you picked which room you like, kids? Obviously, the big one is for me and your dad."

Niamh jumps in first. "I want the one on the top floor."

"What about you, Finn?"

"She can have it. I want the blue one at the back, it's bigger anyway."

I'm pleasantly surprised to avoid refereeing a fight. "Come on, everyone, finish up, it's been a long day and you've got school tomorrow."

We all sleep well, despite being on mattresses. Patrick comes and kisses me on the cheek.

"I'm going to leave a little earlier, love, lots to catch up on with being off yesterday."

"OK, but please don't stay late. I've taken a couple of hours off this morning to get them up and out."

He kisses me on the forehead. "I won't, and good luck."

Niamh is stomping around and sighing dramatically. "Mum, I need my tennis racquet for today. Where is it?"

"I already put it in the car." I catch her out of the corner of my eye, leaving the kitchen. "Niamh! Don't walk away, I was answering you."

"Mum, what are you talking about? I'm behind you."

"Oh, sorry, love, there's just a lot going on. Come on, let's get you out of here."

I wave them out the door and I'm delighted that I have an entire hour to myself before I have to leave. I see movement again from the corner of my eye but when I turn there's nothing there. It's probably just my hair. I'm desperate for a haircut. I tie my hair up, but it happens again when I climb the stairs, the corner of the other eye this time. I need to catch up on some sleep.

I grab a quick shower before work, shutting my eyes and washing away all the dust and sweat from yesterday. As I wash my hair, there is a shadow through my eyelids. It looms and waves, like a tree blocking the sun. When I open my eyes, there is nothing. Maybe I need to get my eyes checked. As I get ready, I have a lovely warm feeling, like the house was made for us.

I grab my keys and run to the car.

"Hello."

I look up and there is a silver-haired lady at the bottom of the drive, smiling and waving.

I open the car door. "Hello there, so sorry, I'd love to stop but I'm just on my way to work, have a good..."

She wanders over. "It's lovely to see a family in this house, just lovely." She seems almost teary with happiness.

"Oh, yes, thank you. We really love the house."

She continues to smile warmly. "Then you must stay."

I really need to leave. "Don't worry, after what we've paid, we'll be living here forever." She reaches out and gently touches both my forearms. Her eyes are still teary, and I'm worried she will start crying.

"She's only curious, you know. She is happy you are here."

I have no idea what is happening, but I am going to be late.

"It was lovely to meet you, but I do..."

She grips my arms a little too hard. "Just let her stay where she feels safe." She reaches her cool, wrinkled hand to my face and touches the corner of my left eye. "Right here, that's where you'll see her. She's happy there."

I look back over my shoulder at the house.

"Don't look directly at her, she doesn't like that."

I shudder and want to get away as quickly as possible, I feel lightheaded. "I..."

"Don't be afraid, dear, Betsy brings warmth."

I want to get in my car more than anything, but I haven't moved an inch.

She squeezes my hands softly. "Yes, you'll all be very happy here."

I nod. My brain can't find any words and my mouth is too dry to say them anyway.

"As long as you don't try to leave, of course."

She turns and walks away, and I get in the car. My hands tremble as I dial Patrick's number.

"Hello. Patrick McCarthy speaking."

"Patrick, it's Betsy. I think we have to..."

Day 10

Extraordinary

I love my morning walk. Geoff is on his front step as always.

"Enjoy your walk, Percy."

"Always do, Geoff."

Norma doesn't like to go out during the week, but at the weekend we take her chair. I walk three miles before sneaking back into the house. Norma is in pain a lot of the time and needs her rest. The TV is blaring from our bedroom; she watches something about selling houses every morning.

"Just me, Norma."

"Shush, Percy!"

Clearly, I've interrupted at a critical moment. I make toast with marmalade and a pot of tea and tap gently on our bedroom door.

"Am I allowed to interrupt?"

She smiles cheekily at me. "Now is fine but you nearly made me miss which house they chose. That's the whole bloody point of watching it."

I roll my eyes; she takes my hand and squeezes. We sit quietly while her show finishes, sipping tea.

"The doctor is popping in today." I had completely forgotten. "Will you help me fix my face before she gets here? I like to look my best, show her I'm good here with you."

"I'll do my best, Norma." I hold up my rough hands with their stumpy fingers and we both burst out laughing. "These hands are more suited to painting fences than faces!"

I do a pretty good job, if I do say so myself, and she looks happy. I want to tell her she is the most beautiful thing I've ever seen without any makeup, but I don't talk like that and I think it would scare her.

"You scrub up well, Norma." I kiss her on the cheek.

"Tidy downstairs for the doctor, will you?"

"Yes, love."

Doctor McBride knocks at the door.

"Good morning, Doctor."

"Good morning, Mr King, how are you both?"

"Good. Tea?"

"Not for me, thanks, I'll get straight up to Norma."

I follow her upstairs. Norma is sitting up proudly in her chair, and she looks a picture, radiant and strong.

"Morning, Doctor, I hope he offered you something to drink?"

"Yes, he did, thank you. I'm good."

The doctor and Norma chat, there are questions and she answers. I don't understand a lot of it. I know I could if I tried but my heart starts to race if I see Norma's face fall. I nod along, as it's important to Norma.

At the door, Dr McBride hands me a piece of paper.

"These are Norma's new tablets; will you pick them up?"

"Yes, of course, I'll do it this morning." There is silence. I think she's waiting for me to ask something, but I already know more than I can handle.

"I'm sorry things aren't going in the direction we'd like, Mr King, but there are still lots of things to try and Norma still seems happy."

I smile. "That's all that matters," and I mean it, that's all that has ever mattered.

I see the doctor out and grab my coat. "Going to get your new pills, Norma, need anything else while I'm out?"

"No thanks, love, but be back in time for cards. I'm not going to let you win this week." I hear her laugh to herself and I laugh, too. I don't know where she finds her strength.

We play cards until bedtime; she beats me easily and doesn't hold off on gloating. I kiss her goodnight and go through to the spare room. I don't sleep properly in here, but they say it's better for her.

"Night, Norma, call me if you need anything."

"Night, love you."

"Love you, too." I climb into bed, another day done. If we are lucky, tomorrow will be much the same. They are the best of days and I never want them to change.

I hear her voice. "Percy." I jump out of bed as fast as my body will allow.

"What? You OK?"

Her eyes look big and shiny. "I'm so sorry about all of this, I'm so sorry you have to spend your days like this." Her eyes start to spill over. It's the first time I've ever seen her cry about it. How do I tell her that I can't think of a better way to spend my days, that the forty-one years we've been together have simply been the most wonderful gift, that I can't believe my luck that I have a woman as amazing as her and I don't think I know how to breathe without her?

"Don't be silly, Norma, I'm fine." I take her hand and kiss it gently and she squeezes it. She knows. She pats the empty side of her bed and I tuck in under the covers.

"Night, Percy."

"Night, Norma."

Day 11

Work from Home

"Good morning." I keep my head down. I don't know what mood she's going to be in. She stops in the middle of the kitchen and it strikes me how small and frail she looks.

"Mark, I'm so sorry, it's just work and you know, I promise... I'm really sorry."

There's no point pretending. "I know, it's OK, I know you've got a lot on."

Her face broadens and she skips over to me, throwing her arms around my neck. I'm happy to see the real Luna. The Luna from last night is an imposter. My Luna is kind and beautiful and loves me.

"Got to rush, honey." She kisses me firmly on the lips. There is a strong taste of mouthwash, but the kiss is wonderful. "I'll pick us up something nice to eat on my way home." She waves and smiles as she leaves me for the day.

I work at home; she thinks it's a joke that I don't leave the house and still call it work. I love it and make great money, but Luna says I've become fat and lazy. She's always yelling at me and telling me she hates me. I know it's her boss that she hates, but when I tried to talk to her about it she broke my nose. I can handle it; she doesn't mean it and people would think I'm ridiculous anyway. She's so small and everyone loves her.

I hear the door slam and her pouring wine; I want to hide here in my office, but I know that won't end well, so I may as well get it over with. She is leaning over the kitchen counter, and I can see anger radiating from her. I focus on maintaining eye contact. Her mouth scares me, almost a snarl. I slip up and she catches me looking at the empty glass in her hand. Her lips curl higher and as she yells, spit and bile spew from her once soft and beautiful mouth.

"Don't!" I try to stop it, but there is no controlling it - it will happen whatever I say or do.

"I'm not..."

"The least you can do, Mark, is be supportive, rather than constantly criticising me and making out I'm an alcoholic."

"I..."

"You what? You don't know shit, Mark, you don't know what I have to deal with. You just sit here on your fat arse doing fuck all every day while I'm doing everything."

I say nothing. There is no point. She won't listen and I'll be wrong anyway. I want to tell her that I earn good money, that I know she hates her job and she should leave and do something she loves, that I miss her, the real her. But any of that would be wrong, very wrong, and she would make me pay.

"Just say nothing as usual then. I've had it! You know I deserve so much better than you? You're a waste of space, always have been." She seizes the bottle of wine and slams the door on her way out to sit on the patio with her phone. I don't follow her. Every decision I make is wrong, but this at least feels like the safest choice. There is little food in the house, but I make do and cook tea. I don't want to make things any worse.

I tiptoe outside. "I made some food if you're hungry." She ignores me, which is better than having it thrown back at me.

I hear her stumble into bed shortly after 1am. She doesn't get undressed and passes out on top of the covers. I think I can smell vomit. I want to help her more than anything, but I am scared and way out of my depth. I feel lost and ashamed. Several hours later, she wakes suddenly, shouting, and sits up straight in bed. She has nightmares most nights, but she won't talk about it. I've tried.

I wake before her and make myself tea. I hear her run to the bathroom and my heart races. I hate waking up every morning and not knowing what to expect.

Her voice is quiet and childlike. "Good morning, Mark."

"Hi, how are you feeling?"

"Like shit. But I guess I deserve that. I'm so sorry, Mark."

"It's fine, I know you're stressed."

"I really am, but I promise I am going to sort it all out today. Tonight will be different, I promise."

She skips over to me. As always, her guilt gone, she's ready to start a new day.

"I love you."

"I love you, too, Luna."

She rushes out of the door and suddenly it hits me like a train. I can't believe I've been so blind. It's déjà vu. It's not that I don't know how she'll react every morning, or what mood she will be in when she comes home, it's that it's the same, exactly the same, every single day. It's so obvious, I can't believe I haven't seen it. Every day will be exactly the same until one of us ends up really hurt, or worse. But I'm worried I'll ruin her life if I speak out.

I grab the essentials and walk out. I don't know where I'm going but I know I can't be here when she gets home. The Luna I love won't come back if I do nothing, and I am just as much to blame if I stand by and watch it happen. I feel like a traitor, but I also feel exhilarated, and fear has been replaced by relief. I want my life back; I need some help.

Day 12

Another Look

"Hi, Fran, so lovely to see you again." She's one of my regulars, every six months without fail. She's sent plenty of business my way, too, so I keep her sweet. She's clearly upset today.

"Hi, Seraphine, you don't know how much I need to see you today. I've so many questions."

"Come in, my dear." My real name is Susan, but that doesn't conjure up the image I'm going for. I've been doing this for over a decade; it's amazing how vague you can be, and these people eat it up. It's not clairvoyance at all, it's counselling. They are all so unhappy, but I bring them hope.

"Sit down, Fran, and put both hands out in front of you on the table. We'll have five minutes of silence so I can see if anyone wants to come through. Just to remind you, I am a sensing medium, I don't see spirits or hear their voices, but I get a sense of what they want to tell you. I try my best not to interpret these messages, just to convey them to you exactly as they are."

I assess her mood and try to remember what was said last time. I know she has a son and is fed up with her husband. Usually I give her a few compliments and reassure her things will get better. Easy money. She seems a bit teary and shaky today, and I wonder if they've had a fight.

"Fran, there are two people who have come to see you today. They tell me you've got a lot going on, that you're overwhelmed and underappreciated."

"Well, yes, that's true, but who is it?" She sounds unusually irritated and impatient today.

"Sometimes they don't tell me who they are, they just pass on messages to you from the spirit world. They tell me you're going through some upheavals and everything feels like it's in limbo, that you feel stuck." She doesn't seem herself. Normally she's nodding along enthusiastically, the typical unappreciated, overworked wife and mother, but something is different.

"They say something big has happened and it's changed you."

She perks up, I'm on the right track.

"Something unexpected has knocked you off your feet." She nods along, and I can see tears loosening in her eyes. I need to be careful here. I don't ever want to hurt anyone.

"Isaac." The name pops into my head and I say it out loud before I have time to think.

She starts to sob. "Isaac... my brother... he died last week."

She must have told me his name before, but I don't remember. I let her continue in between bursts of tears.

"He was in a bar... two men were fighting, he got caught up in it and..."

She can't finish her sentence and I pass her a tissue. I've done this many times. I know she needs comfort, to hear that he's at peace, that there was no suffering.

"He is so glad you are here."

She smiles through her tears.

"He is so proud of you and he is always there if you need him. You can talk to him anytime, he will always watch over you."

She is crying happy tears now; people may call me a fake but I'm helping people.

"Thank you, Seraphine, thank you so much."

Something pops into my head and out of my mouth the same as before. "You need to look in Mum's teapot."

She looks shocked. "I've looked in Mum's teapot plenty of times. It's empty. Why, what is it?"

I don't have anything else for her. "I think he wants you to have another look." I finish with the usual positive messages about moving forward, that there will be a big but welcome change in your life, someone you know will fall pregnant etcetera. I never offer the clients the chance to ask questions in case they come up with something too specific, but today I feel an urge.

"Fran, do you have any questions for your spirit guides? They may not answer but we can ask." That should cover me.

Without hesitation, she asks, "Will I ever have another baby?"

Before I even have chance to digest the question, I answer it and I'm shocked at what I say. I never tell clients what to do. I worry it will come back and bite me.

"Yes, but not with that snake."

She recoils like I've struck her. "Seraphine! How can you say that?" She stands to leave, and she looks furious.

"I'm so sorry, Fran! It wasn't me; it was the spirits and it came out of my mouth before I knew it. Please forgive me."

She is visibly shaking, and she throws money at me before marching out the door.

I have no idea what just happened. I text to cancel my remaining client and opt for a bath and a stiff drink. Eventually I relax and settle down to watch TV. I can't explain what happened today, but I hope Fran is OK. My phone pings with a text.

"I found my mum's diamond jewellery taped to the inside of the teapot. I'm so sorry I stormed out. I know he's awful, but I didn't have any money to make it on my own, until now. Thank you x."

I feel overwhelmed and very sure I don't deserve any thanks. I go to reply but I'm shocked to see I already have. "Everything will be fine, Francie, be brave and I will keep you safe, all my love, Ikey."

She messages back immediately, "That means the world. Thank you so much for everything xxx."

I think I need another drink.

Day 13

Look and You Will Find

He's been at the front door for ages. The door is shut, and he is speaking to someone on the front step. I can't quite make it out, but I know it's a woman's voice, and he sounds pissed off. He storms back in and I pretend I'm checking through the mail.

"What was that?" I continue to flick through the envelopes.

"Nothing, just a persistent salesman."

"Oh, OK, yes, *she* did sound persistent."

He shakes his head and walks past me.

"Samuel?"

"Look, it's nothing, can we just forget about it and go and open some more wedding presents?"

He's distracted all evening. It's completely unlike him and it puts me on edge. We eat dinner and he is as attentive and wonderful as always, but there's something there, something behind his eyes. I might be mistaken but it looks like fear.

"Samuel, I don't want to be a pain and I will believe you if you look me in the eye. Is there anything wrong? Are you in trouble? We are married now. I want to be here for you."

He leaves his chair, kneels at my feet as though proposing marriage and holds my face with his strong hands.

"Mercy, I love you. Everything is fine, I am the luckiest man in the world, and I couldn't be happier. Now, let's go upstairs and celebrate."

He kisses me deeply and insistently and scoops me up in his arms. I believe him.

It's 7.45am, his phone is buzzing in his jacket pocket and has been for the last 20 minutes. Someone really wants to speak to him. It could be an emergency but answering his phone while he's in the shower seems like the wrong thing to do. I knock on the bathroom door.

"Sam! Your phone has been ringing for ages. Do you want me to answer it?"

He answers very casually, "No, don't worry about it, I'll be out in five."

"OK, but it's really annoying. What if it's an emergency?"

"Sorry, baby, I'll get out now."

It's finally stopped. I can't resist looking at the screen, but I have to be quick before he comes out of the bathroom. It's a mobile number I don't recognise and there are 25 missed calls. That's not normal. I jot down the number and put the phone back. Something isn't right - my husband is definitely lying to me, and I need to find out why.

I'm getting paranoid. I am convinced somebody followed me when I was driving to work but they disappeared just before I parked. I need to talk to Samuel tonight, and I won't take no for an answer.

"Excuse me." I look up and there is a woman. She looks and is dressed like me, and it throws me off for a minute.

"Yes?"

She looks nervous. "I don't know how to say this..." She trails off and looks at the ground.

"I'm sorry, do I know you?"

"No... You shouldn't have married him, he's not who he says he is."

"What?"

"He was married to me. He took everything and left me with nothing."

"I'm sorry, you've clearly got the wrong person. Samuel hasn't been married before."

She laughs and my initial pity turns to anger, but my creeping insecurities about Samuel's recent behaviour make me let her continue.

"I made such a mistake; I don't want the same things to happen to you. I'm sorry I laughed, but you took me by surprise. His name isn't Samuel, it's Solomon."

It's my turn to laugh.

"Esther, my name is Esther. You can tell him..."

I put my hand up. "You've had your say. Stop. I can see you've had a tough time but it's not us you're looking for. Trust me, it's not. Now, leave me alone. I mean it."

I see a flash of anger in her eyes, but I am more than a match for her, and I don't break her stare.

"He'll take everything from you, too."

I have had enough now. "I thought you were just mistaken but clearly you're crazy. Say one more word and you'll regret it."

I turn and walk away and when I look back, she is gone, crazy bitch.

It bugs me all morning but eventually I forget about her. I don't text or call Sam. He doesn't need to know. I'm relieved when the day is over, and I can go home. I want to see Sam; I need some reassurance. He always goes for a drink after work on Thursdays, so I'll have to wait a little longer tonight. I see the note on my car in the distance fluttering in the wind. I know it will be from her. She has written the name, Solomon Hart, and an address. The note finishes with, "Just look and you will find." How dramatic. I hate this woman with a passion.

I get home and do exactly as she suggested. I hate myself for it but I don't want to start my marriage off with suspicion and I know it will hurt

Sam if I bring this up. What exactly would I say anyway? "Umm, are you actually someone else?" This is crazy bullshit, but I need to put it to bed properly. I won't have it ruining my marriage.

There's nothing to find, I knew it. He has photos and memories saved and the same paperwork and bills as everyone else; he isn't hiding anything. I have to put everything back where I found it. I can't have him knowing I snooped like this, as it would devastate him.

There is a photograph of his late mother on his bedside table. I'd love it to break accidentally on purpose. I always feel like she's watching and judging me. I hadn't noticed before, but the photo has something behind it that looks like a smaller photo tucked in. I gently take the photo out and there it is, the thing that she warned me about, the thing that I hoped with every fibre of my being didn't actually exist. But it's here in my hand, and there's no pretending or escaping it now. It's a passport for Solomon Hart and it has Sam's picture on it. I have never wanted to smash the photo frame more than I do right now, but I put it back carefully and hide the passport inside my laptop bag. I need time to think.

He is later than usual. I ignore him as he walks into the bedroom, then he sees the photo on the bedside table and his head sinks. I am no one's fool, and there's no talking his way out of this one.

"I already have a bag packed. I'm better than this, Sam, Solomon, whatever your name is!"

He grabs me as I reach for my bag, "Mercy please, just listen I can expl..."

"No, Sam, you lied to me, how could you!"

I have never heard him raise his voice and it frightens me. "I did it to protect you, to protect us."

Tears stream down my face and, even though I hate him for lying to me, I have to know what is going on. I sit down and let him continue.

"My name is Solomon. Just wait, I can explain. Was it Esther?"

I can't believe the crazy bitch was right. I feel so stupid. "Yes, Sam... what? Who is...?"

"She's dangerous, Mercy, stay away from her, I mean it."

He grabs the photo of his mother and holds it tight to his chest and starts to sob. I have never seen him like this, and it breaks my heart.

"Her brother murdered my mother. He didn't know her, it was a robbery gone wrong. I changed my name and moved away because she was threatening me."

He looks terrified and I can see the grief come flooding back. I can't imagine how hard it must have been for him to keep this to himself.

"I've been so scared of her finding us. I thought I'd covered everything, but obviously not. I am so sorry, Mercy, we'll have to leave."

I hold him tight. "No, we don't, Sam."

"Mercy, you don't understand..."

"I've met Esther, and I am more than a match for her. There are things I clearly didn't know about you, but there are things you don't know about me either."

I feel his big, muscular body trembling against me. I won't let her hurt him again, we will be fine; I will fix it.

Day 14

New Brain

My name is Vinnie. A few months ago I couldn't have told you that and, even now, I have to remind myself sometimes. Today is my first day back at work. I can't really do my job, but they can't really sack me either. I bet they wish they could. Before our crash, I used to run a printing machine here. It's pretty dangerous, and I always thought that's how I'd end up hurting myself. My boss knocks on my office door. I didn't used to have an office, I don't really know what it's for.

"How's it going, Vinnie?" He is fiddling a lot; he doesn't usually do that, and I can't concentrate on his face. I banged my head in the crash, but I was lucky, my girlfriend lost an arm and a foot. Still, I banged my head good, and my brain is a bit different.

"Not sure yet, boss, only been here five minutes." He is still twiddling and fiddling his hands, and it makes me want to punch him. I hope I don't have to put up with this level of weirdness forever. My new brain won't keep things in that want to come out.

"I don't want any sympathy, boss, and stop fiddling." My new brain doesn't get embarrassed either. I've learned people don't like that but the things that seem to bother people are actually the things that I like. He puts his hands behind his back. I wonder if he's still twiddling them.

"Sorry, Vinnie, how's Vanessa doing?"

"Not too bad, boss, just don't try and give her a high five!" I laugh and he is horrified. I wonder whether I should tell him about my new brain and how it can't have a quiet joke inside my head anymore. I think I've told him anyway that I'm basically a toddler. I can see he wants to get as far away from me as possible and that's fine by me. I need to see what my new job at this computer is like and, if he stays any longer, my new brain will tell another joke just to make things worse.

I have to make it up to Vanessa, too. I've made too many shitty jokes about her missing parts. "What do you call a woman with one leg? Eileen!" Get it? It doesn't bother me; I'd love her if she was a head on a stick. She says I don't have empathy and I'm sure she's right.

I hate working at a computer. I miss my big, noisy printing machine, I miss the smells and the chat. I think I'll go and see everyone.

It's not right, everyone is different. I know I'm different, but they shouldn't be. Big Pete looks really nervous. I'm not stupid, I'm not going to go near the machines, I know what the yellow lines mean. I think about saying, "Boo." It would be funny but what if someone falls into one of the machines? I would feel bad about that. I see my old supervisor Bagsy approaching. Mustn't call him that, seriously, mustn't call him that.

"Boo!" Nobody laughs and I hear a bit of whispering. I was right, it is funny. I fail to stop myself laughing out loud. I'm basically a toddler.

"What are you up to, Vinnie?" He's being fake nice; I appreciate the effort, but I don't like it.

"I don't like being on my own at my desk. I'm bored, I like it out here. I won't touch anything, promise."

"You can't be here, it's not safe."

I'm standing behind the yellow line. Anyone can walk here; I point at the line.

"No, sorry, Vinnie, I mean _you_ can't be here."

"Then why am I even here!" Even my old brain thought he was a jobsworth; I'm lucky I've never been a violent or angry person, and this hasn't really changed with my new brain. I don't think I am even as angry as I should be about it all.

"Vinnie, please, let's go somewhere quiet."

"Piss off, Bagsy, you can't just stick me in a room on my own."

I hear a few stifled giggles; I shouldn't have said that out here.

"Actually, Vinnie, we can. Let's go, now."

I've been fooling myself. I can't do the job I love and they are only pandering to me because they have to. I look around. Nobody is the same and they won't ever be, so best to leave before they make me.

"Keep in touch, lads. I'll see myself out, Mr Bagson."

I'm going to have to go and tell Vanessa I've been a naughty boy at work now. She'll be one-armed and dangerous. Must try and avoid the jokes. I can't get myself sent home from work and out of the house on the same day. Texting is safer.

"I said some stupid stuff at work, and they want me to come home."

She responds immediately. "You idiot... you OK? X"

"I don't want to sit in an office on my own. I called him Bagsy to his face."

"Ha ha! I'd clap but well, you know... xx"

I laugh out loud. Now I can't wait to get home. That was exactly what I needed. Another message comes through.

"I thought I'd get in first. Come home xx."

"Can't wait. Love you. Let's hold hand when I get home!"

Week Three

We are halfway!

You've read every day for two weeks; the hardest part is done, getting started. Now we just need to continue.

Have a think about what you read last week. Was there a story you preferred, one that got you thinking or is still playing on your mind? Is there a character that you identified with or made you feel something?

Non-fiction books teach us things about the world, but I think that stories teach us about ourselves and what is important to us. The different stories might help you choose what kind of books you may want to read in the future.

But first, let's jump into Week Three, where all the stories are between 1000-1500 words.

Have fun!

Day 15

Jane

There is a car blocking my drive, there is nowhere else to park and it is pissing it down. After the day I've had, I could scream. I feel it pulsing behind my ears and eyes as I park at the end of the road. I know it's stupid, but I am so pissed off.

When I arrive at the bottom of our drive, I recognise the car immediately. It belongs to the new couple who have moved in three doors down. I say new, but I think it's probably been a year since they moved in and I've never even said hello to either of them. My anxiety is off the scale at the thought of confronting them, and I have a weird sense that this is a life-changing moment.

I stand and look at the door for a couple of seconds. Eventually I knock and, instead of politely introducing myself to my neighbour and explaining the mildly annoying situation with their car, I jump straight up on my high horse and practically yell, "Your bloody car is blocking my drive."

I stand there shaking and continue my unnecessary verbal diarrhoea.

"I could be elderly or disabled or have triplets and need to park on my drive for safety."

"Are you? Or do you?" she says calmly, and with a slight look of amusement on her face.

"That's really not the point, is it? It's my drive and I should be able to drive my car on and off it whenever I choose, and your selfish car is blocking it!"

I could literally die of embarrassment. Firstly, I have entirely lost my shit over something that couldn't matter less, and I've followed this up with the words "selfish car".

She is standing in her doorway, a large glass of white wine in her hand, head slightly tilted to one side and the look on her face has changed to one of warmth and sympathy. I stop my ranting and look down at my feet.

"It doesn't matter, I'm sorry." I turn slowly and begin my walk of shame to my house. Halfway down the path, she calls after me, "That's not my car, it's my ex-husband's car."

I keep walking.

"And you're right, he parks just like the inconsiderate prick that he is."

She laughs heartily at her own joke. I hear her quietly shut the door behind me and I run to my house as quickly as humanly possible. I fumble for my keys and unlock the door. In the mirror, I am white-faced and panicked, with water dripping down my face. Why can't I just do things normally? I need a glass of wine and then to work out what to do next.

Hiding indefinitely from shame doesn't seem like an option for any self-respecting adult. I grab a bottle of sparkling rosé from the fridge and a tumbler from the cupboard. I'm shaking so much that I don't trust myself with a wine glass.

There is a knock at the door. Whoever it is can go away, as my track record at exchanges with strangers in the last hour is fairly terrible. Another knock, then I hear the letterbox open.

"I know you're in. Open the bloody door. It's the least you can do after your shouting performance."

"Shit." What the bloody hell do I do now?

She presses the letterbox again several times.

"Open up."

I walk to the door to meet my fate. She is still wearing the beautiful, soft grey loungewear she had on earlier, but has swapped her sheepskin slippers for a pair of very bright trainers and has a gorgeous navy-blue raincoat on over the top. She is holding the large glass of wine in her hand and has the remainder of the bottle under her arm.

"I'm Jane. Looks like you could use a drink." She holds the bottle aloft and waits for my response. I'm mute and fairly sure my mouth is gaping unattractively. I step back and she takes this as an invitation into the house.

"Bloody horrible out there. Good job you've got a drive to park on, otherwise you'd be soaked." She throws her head back and laughs at her own joke for the second time. As she walks past me, she stops and looks me straight in the eye. "Let's get that drink. I guarantee you'll feel better."

It's weird that she's in my kitchen. She spies my bottle and tumbler on the kitchen counter. "Put that one back in the fridge for later and, for goodness sake, get yourself a decent glass."

She pours.

"Thank you." I look down but she finds my eyes.

"Let's drink then."

"Sure." I take a sip.

"No." She lifts her large glass and drinks it all at once.

"Drink it." She mimes downing the glass again. I lift my glass and begin to drink. I get halfway and realise I've misjudged this somewhat. The wine is coming up onto my cheeks and nose but as I go to lower my glass, she puts the tips of her fingers gently on the bottom. I half-drink, half-splutter my way through the rest and eventually put the glass down with wine on my face, up my nose and with my eyes streaming. We burst into fits of laughter.

I laugh with my eyes closed until my belly hurts and my eyes stream even more. Eventually we calm down and she gets the remainder of the bottle.

"That was the funniest thing I've seen in ages!" She laughs again and shakes her head.

"You feel better, right? I knew you would."

Without a doubt, she was right. I feel a lot better and I don't think it is simply the booze. I still feel ridiculous about my behaviour.

"I'm so sorry, I'm not usually anything like that at all. I'm horribly shy and would never shout at anyone! I feel so ridiculous."

"Don't worry yourself, seriously. I get cross all the time and shout at lots of people, so we are balancing the universe out. It's fine, we are all human."

I nod; she makes so much sense.

"What made you do it though? Most times when people do things like that, it's not about the thing that's happening. Do you know what I mean? There's always something deeper making you unhappy."

I know exactly what she means.

"Unless you really are someone who gets mega-pissed about not being able to get on your drive?"

I laugh and roll my eyes. I don't really want to get into it and thankfully she keeps talking.

"Sometimes things go exactly as they are supposed to, the universe wanted us to meet like this today and so it shifted everything to make it so. Maybe we both needed something in our lives. I've just been through a monstrous divorce and you are clearly going through some sort of early midlife existential crisis, which I can't wait to hear all about once you take the stick out of your ass and start talking to me!"

She laughs and reaches to put her hand on mine. It's a level of personal contact that I'm not usually comfortable with. She senses it immediately.

"Don't worry, I won't try and give you a hug yet!"

The evening passes in a blur of laughter and stories. What happened on her doorstep feels like it happened to two completely different people. The two people sitting here are just Catriona and Jane, two new friends getting to know each other.

"I'm starting to think I'm here tonight to teach you how to be more open and less worried. Maybe try just being you?" She looks me straight in the eyes. "I won't judge you, you know."

It's like she knows, although I know she can't. I've never uttered anything out loud. I open my mouth to speak and then shut it. I shake my head very slightly; I can tell she understands.

"I'm here when you're ready, and you will be."

I hope she's right.

Day 16

Happy Again

I am sitting on the floor inside our wardrobe. I am here because I have been bad. I deserve to be here; I am a terrible wife and he deserves so much better. I used to have all my clothes hung up in here, but now my side is empty. I am not allowed any of those clothes anymore. They are too good for me. I have these shapeless clothes now and I am not allowed to choose for myself. I understand though, and I am happy to wear them. They help me learn my lesson. I can get my beautiful clothes back one day, but I must be good.

I could come out. Elliot is at work and he would never know, but I can't risk it. If he walks in the house and sees I have been in the kitchen or lounge, there will be hell to pay. I do not want the police here again. They don't believe me anyway, they believe him and then I find myself in even more trouble. He will be back in four hours, so I can last without food and drink until then. I try to scrape my name into the wall with my nail. I used to have beautifully manicured nails, but I don't deserve those anymore. I have to keep my nails plain and short. I used to be beautiful, but I am a mess now. We were so in love and I know we will get back there, I know we will be happy again, I just need to behave myself.

I know where it all went wrong. We tried to have a baby, but I am broken inside. He deserves to have a child and I am unable to give him one

- wouldn't that make anyone angry? I think it excuses everything. If you feel angry and let down by the world, of course you are going to lash out; I don't see why it's a problem. The important thing is that we get back to normal, it doesn't matter what has happened before. I lie on the floor and I wait for him to come home. I want to be right here when he comes in.

I hear the front door and the tail end of a telephone meeting; he works so hard for us. I stand up and straighten myself the best I can. I want to look my best. I peer through the gap between the doors and I hear him come up the stairs. He sits on the edge of the bed, loosens his tie and drapes his coat carefully over the chair in the corner of the room. He looks agitated. I hope he hasn't had a bad day. He reaches out and opens my door, and I smile warmly at him. I want him to know how pleased I am to see him, I want to make him happy. Our eyes meet, but he is not happy, he screams and stumbles backwards towards the bed.

"Alice, what the fuck are you doing here?"

He grabs for his coat, finds his phone, and starts to frantically press the screen. I sigh. I was afraid of this.

"Elliot, please, let's talk."

He is fumbling with his phone and cursing under his breath. "How did you get here? Did they let you out?"

I look down at my shapeless hospital pyjamas and laugh.

"You can't be here, Alice, there's a restraining order, shit, oh shit!"

He is clearly panicking but he seems to have successfully dialled a number and puts the phone to his ear. This is not going to plan at all.

"Put the phone down, Elliot." I point the gun at his chest. I have never used a gun before and it feels weird in my hand. I hope it works. I haven't even pressed the trigger yet. I don't want to have to shoot him, but he might leave me no choice. We both know I am capable of pulling the trigger. He puts his hand to his cheek to feel the scar I left with the knife last time. I didn't want to do that either but he really doesn't listen. I will try one last time to be nice.

"Elliot, just listen. I've come to sort things out so we can start afresh, be happy again. Neither of us wants things to be like this between us."

"Are you fucking crazy?"

"That's what they say!" I roar with laughter, but he doesn't laugh. I don't know why, that was funny. He has put the phone down at last and I know I have one last chance to convince him.

"Elliot, I know things haven't been great between us..."

"Alice, there is no us and there hasn't been for almost five years. You need to go back to the hospital. Just put that gun down and let me call them, please."

"We could start again, maybe even adopt. We could be happy again, I know it." He is shaking his head; I have tried everything to convince him and he is just being horrible.

"Alice, please, can I call someone? The hospital or the police? I know you don't want to hurt me." He leans towards me and holds out his hand, but he looks smug and condescending. Now I remember why I stabbed him.

"You're wrong, Elliot, I do want to hurt you." I shoot the gun. "Oh my God, it works!" I am amazed, but I've missed him and hit the wall. He seems frozen to the spot, which is ideal as I get a better shot this time. I shoot him in the stomach. I think that will do it, but it will take a while.

I head downstairs and make myself comfortable on the sofa. I'll give it five minutes and call the hospital. It's quite nice there and if I can't be here, I'm happy to go back. I can hear him thrashing about upstairs. It didn't have to be this way. I find the phone and call the hospital, and when my favourite nurse answers, I try to sound scared.

"Hi, Greg, it's Alice. I blacked out and I just woke up in my old house.

I'm scared. Can somebody come get me?"

I hear a lot of frantic chatter down the phone, but I'm bored now so I hang up. You can get away with pretty much anything if you pretend to be crazy. There is silence upstairs now so I can at least wait in peace until they come and get me.

Day 17

Look Back

I look around the empty house. I won't miss one thing. I hated every second of living here. He chose it, he didn't listen to anything I ever wanted. We lived here for nearly ten years and I still didn't know the rooms in detail. I never felt awake here, I felt like a ghost. I knew he'd leave eventually. I blame the house; it looks better empty. I close the door for the last time and post the keys through the letterbox. I don't look back. Today won't work if I decide to look back.

I've been called in for a meeting by my boss, Jada. She thinks I want to leave, so at least she's noticed something is different. She is a horror of a human being and, alongside the house, she is responsible for my downfall. The fuel light is flashing on my car, but there is just enough to get to work. I won't ever need any more.

At the office there are banners and balloons and stupid printout photos everywhere. Shit, I'd forgotten it was Helen's birthday. I feel bad. I'll never see any of these people again, and most of them don't mean anything to me, but Helen I do like. I eat cake and give Helen a birthday hug, and promise we'll do long-overdue drinks.

"I'm so sorry, Helen, I need to meet Jada. Have a gorgeous rest of the day!"

I blow Helen a kiss as I leave. My meeting is in five minutes and I don't want to be late. I turn my back on the room and I don't look back.

Jada doesn't look up as I knock and enter.

"Sit down please, Vivienne, I just need a minute." Her voice sounds different. She doesn't look up and I stay standing, staring at the solid glass award on her desk. I can't believe my life has actually come to this; it could be over in ten seconds. She looks up and, without thinking, I grab the award with both hands and raise it high over her head. I can hear my heart beating and the blood pulsing through my ears. Hundreds of thoughts rush through my head, threatening to spill out.

On the surface, I know I seem fine, but I want life to end. I want everything to stop. I am angry, and I don't want any ambiguity. I want to tell them why I did it, I want them to know I'm not sorry and that I am happy she is dead. I'm in prison anyway. I'll take what's coming, it will be a walk in the park compared to this.

She has tears in her eyes, but they aren't new. Her makeup is smeared, and her eyes are puffy and red. She doesn't look scared and that terrifies me. I don't move.

"Do it!"

For a minute I think I will. This woman has terrorised me and I should be glad she's crying.

"Go on, do it! You'll be doing me a favour, I deserve it." Her shoulders start to shake, and she sobs violently. She is right, she does deserve it and I don't believe this performance for a second. I bring the award down hard and it smashes into dozens of pieces as it strikes her desk. She doesn't flinch and I know instantly that she didn't care whether I did it or not. Despite the noise, nobody comes, and we sit in silence for what feels like hours. One of us will occasionally cry but otherwise we are silent, sitting there amongst the shattered pieces, two shattered people. She is the first to speak and there is alcohol on her breath.

"I've come so far down this road; I don't know how to get back. I hate who I am, I hate how I treat people and I just want everything to stop. I can't see any way out."

I am speechless. I have never seen this woman be anything other than bloodthirsty and vicious. I had no idea she felt this way, I had no idea she felt anything at all. It's like I am seeing her naked. She is holding nothing back, and I can hear the desperation in her voice.

"I'm so sorry about what I've done to you. I have so much hurt and anger inside and dishing it out to other people is all I know."

She starts to cry again, and I join her this time. It's like a release, a relief and we look each other in the eye as we let go of everything. In that moment we know there is another way. We've made a huge mess of our lives, but we don't have to give up. I lean forward and touch her hand.

"I've made the world's biggest fuck up of my life, my husband left because I'm unbearable and I've been blaming everyone and everything since." I am so relieved to say it out loud. I've always known I was equally to blame for the breakdown of my marriage, but I couldn't face it, I needed it to be someone else's fault. Tears continue to spill down her face. I am amazed at how human she looks and disappointed with myself for not looking past what was obviously a front. I couldn't see further than my own problems.

"At least you had a husband, at least someone wanted you. I've never had anyone, ever. Nobody wants me."

"I'm sure that's not..."

"Come on, Vivienne, you know I'm right. I treat people like shit, and they run a mile."

She is right, but the Jada I'm seeing now is quite different.

"Well, I was going to smash your head in not so long ago, so maybe you are right..." We both laugh and cry unashamedly.

"... but you can change all of that, we can both leave this room as different people, support each other and live the lives we deserve. Fuck what we've done so far. Everyone makes mistakes. You don't have to pay for them forever. Are you in?"

She nods and smiles through the tears and I see something wonderful in her eyes. It's hope. Sometimes help comes when you least expect it and I feel relieved and grateful to be alive for the first time in as long as I can remember. That feeling is briefly replaced by panic as I realise that in my desperation I have sold or given away everything I own. Just as quickly, I realise that doesn't matter. What matters is a better life.

Jada and I need to get out of here.

"Let's go and clean ourselves up and go get coffee, shall we?"

Jada smiles but she still looks afraid.

"Jada, I know you are scared. We both have a lot of work to do to get on the right track, but I'm guessing neither of us want to spend the rest of our lives answering for the things we did when we were hurt and lost."

"I know, but I've been so..."

"Then be different, be better. I will help you. We will help each other." She simply nods and we get up to leave. I'm shocked at how brave and strong I feel. I look back at the desk covered in shattered glass and shudder at how this could have ended so differently. I know I won't make the same mistakes again. I nearly lost everything but, rather than seeing it as the end, it's going to be my new beginning.

Day 18

They Can't Save Me

I'm cooking steaks for us; it would be good to have a nice evening for once. Things haven't been right for a while now. I hear him come in the door. I hope he's hungry.

"Can't you put the extractor fan on? It stinks in here."

"Will do, sorry. I don't like to when you're not here. It makes me think someone is going to sneak up behind me."

He rolls his eyes. "You're a total nut job. Who exactly is going to come and attack you at the cooker with the door locked?"

"I know it's stupid. It's just…"

"Give me that, you can't cook steak for shit anyway." He overacts switching the cooker hood on. He is such a prick sometimes.

"Open some wine, would you, if you can manage that."

I suspect this isn't going to be a nice evening but I'm not ready to give up on it yet. I step away and my foot disappears from underneath me. At first, I think he's pushed me. I'm horrified, he's a cantankerous old bastard but never violent. I realise too late that I've slipped on grease. My arms grab out frantically, but they can't save me. He doesn't even hear it happen with the cooker hood on full blast. The last thing I feel is my head and neck striking the counter. I feel the break, deep down inside, everything goes black for the shortest of moments and then all feeling is gone. I'm floating to the ground, the noise of the cooker seems far away somehow and the outline of Ian's back is blurry and his movements slow. He still hasn't seen me and I can't move or talk.

"I can get it my..." He stands on my outstretched arm as he turns to tell me off for being slow with the wine. I don't feel it; it's only at that moment I realise that I'm not really me anymore, I'm just watching. He looks shocked but not upset. He looks scared, terrified in fact, and I think he's also a little annoyed at the mess. He's never had what I would call normal emotions or responses. He's wired up wrong.

"Fuck." He looks around, I'm not sure what for. I thought he might check my pulse but when I look at me again, it's obvious I'm dead. He stops cooking and turns the cooker hood off, then leaps over me and runs into the hallway and out of the front door. I hear the garage open, but he doesn't get into the car. I think I could follow him, but somehow, I know I've got eternity to do that. I think I'll stay here with my body; she won't be around much longer. I don't feel sad about that, and maybe that's part of it all. I hear Ian clattering around. He doesn't seem to have called the police. I hope he's not going to do anything stupid. He's a grumpy old shit with a foul mouth but he'd never have laid a finger on me.

He comes back with a saw, hammer, tarpaulin, bin bags and a rope. He's about to make a huge mistake, and I can't watch. He dumps his makeshift dismembering kit onto the kitchen floor and runs off again. I pray he's coming to his senses. This was an accident, and he's not in any trouble, but the longer he leaves it, and if he does anything other than call the police, he will be. There's no instruction manual that comes with this, but somehow I know what to do.

I close my eyes and pull myself back down. It's like trying to remember something you've forgotten but you know is in your brain somewhere. I feel a shift, I open my eyes again and I'm on the floor. I know I haven't got long to fix this, and I'm definitely dead, but I know I can communicate from here. He comes running back in with a change of clothes for him and my handbag. I don't know what he's thinking. I concentrate again and turn my head towards him. I plan my message very clearly and play it in my head, willing my dead lips to move. "Ian, please, I fell, just call the police, please."

My head is slow, and my neck is broken. It cracks and wobbles towards him, my eyes staring and lifeless. My words come out slow and pained, like a mixture between a growl and a scream. It's a hideous noise and a horrifying sight.

"Ia... Ian..." I see my already terrified husband become struck with horror; he is visibly shaking. No other words will come. I'm not strong enough, I can't hold my head anymore and it hits the floor with a sickening thump. My face is grotesque and twisted from my failed attempts to warn him. He grabs the phone and dials frantically, then shouts down the phone.

"Mum, oh Mum, help, please help!"

Oh no, not that old bitch. Well, at least it beats watching yourself be chopped up and put in plastic bags. He runs out of the room and I wait. I start to feel lighter, the room starts to blur a little more, I can still see everything but I know I'm getting ready to leave and I know that where I'm going is good. I can feel warmth and a kindness upon me. I don't know how long I wait; I don't feel time passing. The room is a blur now and I feel myself slipping away towards the kind and gentle place that is waiting for me. I know I can leave; he's getting help and he'll be fine. I hear him crying and I can sense his mother in the room with him. She'll make sure he's OK. I hear her voice before I drift into eternity.

"You grab her legs, I'll get her arms. We need to do this in the bathroom. It would be too messy in here."

Day 19

Not Today

I tell my friends I prefer the train. I hate the train, but I like to drink. Actually, that's not quite true, I don't like to drink; I just drink. I stay away from the office when I can, but inevitably I have to meet clients. Mouthwash and chewing gum are my friends, and sometimes a couple of codeine to bridge the gap.

A familiar voice cuts through the fog. "Rob, is that you?"

I know him, but I don't know who he is. "Yeah, hi mate! How's it going?"

He is pleased to see me, so I am pleased to see him too. His name won't come through the swamp in my brain.

"Great! You must be doing well for yourself; you look amazing!"

He's right, I am doing well for myself and people always tell me I look amazing. It's weird that my body looks so good. It must be the money.

"Thanks, you look great, too. It's so nice to see you." I'm worried about being any more specific.

"Great to see you, too, Rob. We should meet for a drink sometime?"

Now he's talking. "Sounds great, mate."

"Just give me a call and we'll sort something. Do you still have my number?"

I have no idea. "Yes, I do. I'll message you later."

Despite appearances, I have it all planned out. I'll quit when I'm thirty-five, I won't have knackered my health, I'll have plenty of money and can do something else with my life that isn't so bloody stressful. There's plenty of time, but for now I need alcohol and I have it under control.

As always, I am amazing with the clients, professional, yet personable - they love me. They almost beg me to go to lunch with them. They seem like the "drinking to celebrate a deal" types. Thankfully, I'm right, expensive bottles of wine all round and the food is outstanding.

"If you're ever thinking about a change of career then do let us know, we'd love to have you."

No chance, I'm not swapping one corporate nightmare for another. They can't afford me anyway. "That's very kind, but I love what I do, and now we get to work together so everyone wins!"

We clink glasses and I excuse myself. The level of drinking is polite, to say the least, and I need a top-up in the bathroom.

I open the bottle of vodka in my inside pocket, sit on the toilet seat and drink a quarter of it immediately. I can't drink more than half just now; it needs to last me until quitting time.

My phone has been on silent while I've been schmoozing and there are six missed calls from my assistant. My rule is call once and leave a message. I call her.

"Hello, Rob?"

"Polly, what's the deal with all the calls? And don't answer my phone like that!"

"Rob, I'm so sorry... your father has had a heart attack..."

My face feels funny. I can hear my own breathing as Polly continues to deliver the bad news as well as she can.

"... get there quickly. Where are you and I'll send a car."

"Is he..."

"No, Rob, as I said, he's in A&E. Tell me where you are and I'll send a car to take you there. You need to go now."

My voice is quiet. I'm sure she hasn't heard me like this, but I don't seem able to make it any bigger. "I'm at the High Bar in town."

"Wait outside, it won't be long. I'm so sorry, Rob, I hope he pulls through."

I thank her and, after hanging up, I drink the rest of the vodka in one go and feel momentarily better. I splash my face and put on my best smile. I make vague excuses at the table and leave, collecting high fives and handshakes.

"No rest for the wicked, eh Rob?"

"Got a better offer, Rob, have you?"

I laugh and wink appropriately and leave them to sip their wine.

I need to get there quickly so I can't stop, but if I don't stop, I won't have any alcohol. If I stop, Dad might die before I get there. My head is screaming and I know deep down that although I want to do the right thing, I won't, because I'm not the one in control of my choices anymore.

"Can you pull over here please, mate, I'll be two minutes." I run in and buy a small bottle of vodka. If that's the five minutes that decides whether I see Dad again, I'll have to live with it. I can't even contemplate losing Dad. Mum's been gone almost ten years and to this day I have never allowed myself to believe it.

I run from the taxi to the ward, trying to make up what I lost. There's an exhausted looking nurse at the front desk.

"Hi, I'm Robert Green, my dad is here, he's Robert Green, too."

Her smile worries me, it seems to be more pity than anything. "I'll find the nurse who's looking after him. Wait over there, Mr. Green."

Another exhausted nurse leads me to Dad. She warns me about the scary machines, but it still hits me like a ton of bricks. He looks frail, which seems impossible for a man of his size.

Her voice is kind and gentle. "He's stable, we are going to do some..."

I need to get out. "I'm sorry, I need a minute."

"I understand, Mr. Green, but you may want to come back as soon as possible. Your father is very unwell."

I run to the nearest toilet and panic takes hold when I realise the bottle is gone. Uncontrollable anger rises inside me. I bang my fists on the mirror and kick over the bin, pull at my hair and my face in desperation, and then fall over the bin I've just kicked. I feel frantic and hopeless. There will be no booze for sale in the hospital, and I've no codeine left. I know this is beyond selfish and the consequences may be catastrophic.

I pull myself together to speak to the receptionist. "Hi, can you tell me where's the closest place I can get a bottle of champagne?"

"Ooh, lovely! Are we celebrating?"

"Yes, indeed!" Inside I am dying. I wish I were better but I'm not.

"There's nothing, I'm afraid You can get chocolate or flowers at the gift shop though? Nearest supermarket is a twenty-minute drive, at least."

Dread rips through me as I realise I am going to have to go without. I can't let Dad die alone. I sit by Dad's bed; I'm sure he doesn't even know I'm here. I'm assured the doctor will be here any minute. I've been horrible to the nurses, and there's no excuse but I'm crawling inside and can't keep it together. I hate myself for it but I'm starting to wish he'd just die so I can go. I have become a complete monster. How have I ended up this way?

A group of doctors come in. One is clearly the boss and he is flanked by three juniors who barely look old enough to be out of school. He explains what they want to do to my dad. I listen as much as I am able, it sounds awful but they seem to think it will work. He'll make it but it's going to be a long road. One of the baby doctors is looking at me.

"You OK?" he mouths.

I nod. He's clearly placated and continues to take notes. The big doctor shakes my hand and they begin to file out. On his way out, the young one hands me a note and whispers in my ear, "He doesn't care about anything other than stitching people back together or prescribing a drug, but I do."

I don't understand. Clearly my dad needs surgery and drugs. We can't hug his heart better. "What do you..."

He puts his hand on my shoulder and I feel like breaking his wrist. "Things don't have to be like this, but you have to want them to be different."

I resist calling him a prick and I'm relieved when he is gone. His note is a telephone number and, "Addiction is a serious disease, just like a heart attack. You deserve treatment and recovery just as your father does."

If I had alcohol now, I would drink it. I would drink it all. I would want to pour it away with every fibre of my being but, as things stand, it has me, it owns me. I kiss Dad on the forehead, reassured that he will still be here when I return. I make my way home to drink to oblivion. I promise myself I will dial that number tomorrow; I know need to get my power back. Just not today.

Day 20

Some Kind of Monster

I finish my makeup. I'm wearing a stunning, black, fitted dress, and my hair is sitting perfectly around my face as always. I hear my phone ping; the taxi is outside. He wanted to go together but I hate taxi rides with other people.

"Gabrielle?" I nod and the driver smiles. I make sure he won't talk to me but before I do, I catch his eyes and see the familiar flash. Haven't seen that in quite some time, reassuring and unnerving in equal measure. We complete most of the journey in silence, but he's bound to say something. He probably hasn't seen another in years either. He catches my eye again and smirks. "Be good."

"I always am."

He laughs loudly. "I'm not."

I could tell that without him saying so. I text Jesse to let him know I'm arriving soon. He is completely smitten with me, and he likes that I'm not as chaotic and emotional as other women. I don't need to be, I can have things as I want them and I have no insecurities.

We arrive outside the restaurant; I get out without saying anything further to the driver. I was truthful, I am good but, in all honesty, I do prefer the simpler, less civilised days. Jesse runs over. "Hi, babe, you look incredible!"

His eyes are glassy, and his tongue is all but falling out. I love the effect I have on him. I kiss him on the cheek. "Let's go inside, I'm freezing."

He moves to take his coat off to put around me, but I put my hand up to refuse. Of course I'm not actually freezing, it's just a more polite excuse than bored.

"That's sweet," I say, "but let's just go in."

He's going to propose today. He would have done it eventually, but I've moved it forward. It's not against his will - the timing just works better. He gives me everything I need and I can only stay a maximum of ten years. I don't think he's my forever. That's a much bigger commitment for me. There's no "death us do part", but I'd like a wedding and a honeymoon, I like the attention and the beautiful things. Humans are rather ridiculous to an outsider; they never learn, and ideas are rarely new. I want to try my hand at housewife for a bit. I've tried every job and they all bore me. I end up wanting to cause trouble and I know how that has ended in the past.

We sit down at the table and I make small talk. I suspect he won't pop the question until dessert.

"How was your day?"

"Great, I played golf with Dawson, I was rubbish, worst game I've played in..." I smile and nod along as I have to play nice. Despite the perfect packaging, he wouldn't want me if I was unkind. I know I could trick him but this will work much better for me if I'm genuinely wanted. I like that.

"... would you come with us next weekend?"

I don't know what he's asking but I don't want him to know I wasn't listening. "Would you like me to?"

"Of course! I'd love you to do everything with me."

He would, genuinely. "Then I'm in."

I reach out and grab both his hands and look deeply into his eyes, but we are interrupted by the waitress.

"Would you like to order a drink?" I recognise her, and I see a moment of recognition in her eyes, too. I know who she is, but I can tell she's having trouble placing me. I'd rather it stayed that way.

Jesse steps in. "We'll have a bottle of champagne, the Moët, please?"

She writes it down but is still looking at me rather than him. He's too polite but he tries again. "Just the drinks for now, we'll have a look at the menu later."

She comes out of her trance and smiles at him. "I'm so sorry, sir, I just thought for a moment I knew..." She gestures towards me and I cut her off quickly.

"No, I'm afraid we don't know each other." I rarely have to do this as I don't let paths cross. This is simple bad luck, but I'll have to get rid of her. She walks away and Jesse relaxes, shakes his head, and forces a small laugh.

"What was that about?"

"No idea, I must look like someone she knows."

"Nobody looks like you."

I can't argue with him. She's just about to enter the kitchen and I see recognition hit, she turns, and her eyes are full of hatred and fury. She comes stomping back to the table.

"I didn't think it was you... It can't possibly be, it's been thirty years!"

Jesse is justifiably confused, but we both let her continue. "I ended up in jail because of you and have to wait tables now! They believed you rather than me. I'm sure you were very persuasive!"

She is being hysterical which will help.

"You don't look a day older, but I know it's you!"

I can feel the heat rising in me and I have to control myself. I'd love to destroy her right here but it will have to wait. I have to say something though - how dare she ruin my moment.

"How dare you! I have no idea what you are talking about. You are supposed to be serving us, you ridiculous waste of a human being. Now leave us alone!"

Her eyes fill and she waddles away. I can sense I've gone past the imaginary line of social acceptability but at least it's over with. Some people have no sense of time or occasion. I turn and look into Jesse's eyes but somehow, they aren't the same. He's seen something he doesn't like, and he's worried. If I need to, I can talk him around easily. I could even manipulate him daily for the rest of our lives, but I won't. It's nothing to do with his feelings, it just doesn't suit me.

A different waiter comes over with our menus, apologises, and provides a perfect opportunity for me to win this back. I feign shock and upset.

"She accused me of doing something terrible to her thirty years ago. I'm not even thirty years old." I dab away a fake tear. "Everyone makes mistakes. Please tell her there's no hard feelings and that I'm sorry for what I said. I felt threatened and lost my temper for a moment. Please apologise to her for me."

We look at the menu in silence. Why are people incapable of thinking and talking at the same time? They're such simple beings. I'm usually so careful; nothing like this has happened before. I won't feel relaxed until I deal with her, but I have to wait until it's safe.

"Back in a minute, darling." I walk towards the toilet. I need to compose myself. She is in there, splashing her face with water. She looks lost and confused but the anger is still there, threatening to bubble over again.

"I know it's you."

"What is wrong with you? Do I look sixty to you?"

"No... but... how?"

I flash my eyes to frighten her. "Don't ask questions you don't want the answer to." I would dispose of her this second if I didn't think it would compromise me. She runs out of the toilets screaming, and that will work perfectly. At our table, Jesse is speaking to the restaurant manager. I don't get the details but it's clear Jesse is angry and is getting a profuse apology.

"Come on, Gabrielle, we're leaving. She is saying you're some kind of monster. She's clearly unstable."

He points at the manager. "I want her fired."

He's exactly right, she is unstable. I'll deal with it when he falls asleep tonight.

We jump into a taxi, and he says, "Gabrielle, I'm so sorry. That must have been horrible for you. I guess she was just jealous."

I shrug. I'm just grateful we are out of there.

"Gabrielle, this isn't how or where I wanted to do it, but all I know is that I want to be with you forever." He holds out the most beautiful ring. "Will you marry me?"

"Yes!"

He is ecstatic and we hug, I make tears to match his and copy his expressions. Maybe I've been wrong, maybe this one could be forever. We relax in the back of the taxi, wrapped in each other's arms. I lean in and kiss his neck.

Day 21

No Place For Doubt

I am totally in love, but it's not what I was expecting. I imagined warm and fuzzy; instead it's more desperation and anxiety. I see her in line for coffee at least twice a week. I go far too many times hoping to meet her, and I wouldn't sleep if I didn't pour half of it away. I know her name is Leah, at least that's what she asks for on her cup.. The most we have ever said to each other is hello, but it was the best hello ever. I replay it in my head all the time. She is an angel.

Monday morning, 8.30am, there's a ninety percent chance she'll be here. I am excited, and I look as good as I can. I can't believe my luck, she's already in the queue and there's nobody behind her. If there was ever a moment to talk to her this is it. She turns around as I join the queue. She smells amazing, like watermelons and cucumber, and her hair is a frame of curls for her stunningly beautiful face. She takes my breath away. I absolutely ache for her; she is everything.

"Hi." Her voice is even more beautiful than I remember. The anxiety is bubbling in my stomach, but I've practised this a thousand times in the mirror, and I can't miss my chance.

"Hi, I've seen you here a few times. Do you work near here?"

I don't want to sound like a stalker or scare her off, but I need to start a conversation. I can't just say hello and have her smile and turn away, I need her.

"Yeah, just across the street. I love the coffee here." This is it, it's perfect, I can ask her to meet me here for coffee one day.

"Me too, maybe..."

The grumpy teenager behind the counter ruins it for me. I could scream.

"Next, please!"

She flashes me the most wonderful smile and waves before she turns away. The moment is lost. I order my coffee and head off to work. I don't even know where she works. I've contemplated following her but I'm not sure that's how happy relationships begin.

I drop into my seat and thump my bag down on the desk.

"Whoa, Dami, what's with you?" Mabel is my best friend at work, and she has more piercings on her ears and face than I have fingers and toes. Usually I love sitting next to her but even she won't be able to lift my mood today.

"C'mon, D, spill it, what's up?"

I tell her about Leah, she mimes vomiting a few times, but I can't help gushing when I talk about her.

Mabel whispers into my ear, "Do you believe in magic?"

I'm really not in the mood for her shit today. "No, Mabel, can you just leave me alone, please? My life is ruined, and I just want to get to work."

"Fine, fine. Sorry, Dami. Just trying to help a friend in need."

I sulk all morning and eat lunch at my desk. I'm not in the mood for company. I think I'll take a couple of hours of flexitime and head home early. I'd better apologise to Mabel before I go, it's not her fault and I know I was far too short with her earlier. Luckily, Mabel is amazing and hugs me before I even get the chance to apologise.

"Listen, Dami, if this girl is as special as you say she is, then you need to call this number." She hands me a piece of paper with only a number on it. "My friend, Raven. Tell her I gave you this number and you're calling about unrequited love. She will help you."

"Mabel, I don't think..."

"Just do it, Dami, what have you got to lose? Open your stiff little mind a bit and you never know what could happen."

I hug her goodbye. She's right, I am closed-minded but I'm not sure someone named Raven will be the answer to that.

My phone call with Raven lasts all of two minutes. She is surprisingly business-like, takes all my details and what I know about Leah, which is embarrassingly little.

"Are you sure she has no feelings for you? Magic can only be used when the universe is shifting the wrong way."

"She doesn't even know my name, so yeah, pretty sure."

"Very well. I will perform the love spell tonight, at 10pm. At that time, you must be alone and focussed. The spell will only work if it fits with your intentions and desires. There is no place for doubt with magic."

"Ok..."

She cuts me off, "I'm not finished. Within twenty-four hours you must see Leah and say the words, 'our time is now'. That will complete the spell and the universe will take care of the rest. Goodbye, Dami, and good luck."

She hangs up before I answer and doesn't even ask me for money. I thought the point of this sort of thing was to con poor, desperate people like me out of money. I know I am being ridiculous, but I do exactly as she asks and make sure that I am at the coffee shop for 8.30am. Leah has already ordered and is waiting. I can't risk her slipping past me, so I go straight up to her.

"Our time is now." As soon as I say it, I know it is a big mistake. Huge. Her face screws up like there is a bad smell and I can see she wants to run a mile. Although why wouldn't she? What idiot walks up to someone and says shit like that? I'm going to kill Mabel, but I'm a bit scared of Raven so a strongly worded text will have to do. I'm still standing there, saying nothing, feeling like I am the worst. She is clearly confused and definitely pissed off.

"I'm sorry, what did you just say?"

I stutter and fumble and come up with, "Sorry, I meant to ask the time. Do you have it?" She shakes her head and leaves before even collecting her drink. It's over before it even started.

Mabel isn't in today, lucky for her, and I count the seconds until I can go home and wallow in my devastation, the love of my life lost. I am a complete idiot. I can't find the words to text Raven so I call her. What can she do to me down the phone? Plus, I need to vent somewhere, and Mabel is avoiding my calls.

Raven listens to me rant without saying anything for so long that I think she has hung up.

"Hello?"

"Yes, I'm here. Have you finished?" She sounds completely unaffected by my outburst.

"Yes, yes, I suppose so." There's no point, is there? I don't believe in any of this anyway. Obviously my weird behaviour just freaked Leah out. It's not Raven's fault.

"You told me there was no chance she had feelings for you."

"I didn't say *no* chance."

"If you cast a love spell on someone who already loves you, it destroys that love. Of course, all you have to do is reverse it and you'll be back where you started. I can cast a reversal spell at 10pm tonight, all you have to do is..."

I'm not being sucked in by this again. If there's any chance at all with Leah, I need to do it the old-fashioned way and just go and talk to her.

"That's very kind of you, Raven, but you've done more than enough."

"Honestly, it's no trouble at all."

"No, thanks for everything, Raven. Goodbye." I feel better for getting it all off my chest, although I just can't believe I went with any of this in the first place. I get an early night and vow to try and fix things with Leah tomorrow, even if it only means she doesn't think of me as a weirdo anymore.

I am panicking. I've forced myself to go, I'm used to hoping she's there, but today I'm hoping for some reason that she's not. Of course, she's there, and devastatingly, I have never seen her looking more beautiful. She walks straight over to me and I think I am going to swallow my tongue; my palms are sweaty and I would give anything to be anywhere else in the world right now. Weirdly, she is smiling. I smile back but I know it must look odd. I don't feel very smiley and my face isn't working properly. I let her speak first.

"Hi, I am so terribly sorry about yesterday. I don't know what came over me. I am so sorry I was so rude."

I can't believe it; she is apologising to me! I love her even more.

"Don't worry at all, I wasn't my best yesterday either."

She smiles and I almost jump up and down with excitement when she says, "Can I make it up to you? Meet me here for coffee after work?"

It is without a doubt a dream come true. "That sounds fantastic. Five-ish OK?"

"Perfect, see you later." She smiles and brushes past me and her beautiful smell is all around me. Five o'clock feels like an eternity away. I don't know how I'm going to make it through the day. I feel like I owe Raven an apology. I was out of order yesterday. I text her,

"So sorry for my rant yesterday, you didn't deserve it. Take care."

She texts back just as I get to my desk. "I get it, it's hard when you are in love. I only try to help people."

I feel better, she's not offended, and everything has worked out well in the end. I actually feel so much better knowing that I didn't use any tricks to get Leah to go out with me. A second text from Raven comes through.

"But did it work?"

Week Four

Congratulations on completing Week Three! I hope you enjoyed the stories and are getting a better idea of what type of books you would like to read once we've finished this week.

Only seven more days to go and you will have read every day for four weeks. The stories for Week Four are only slightly longer than last week, and you should find 15-20 minutes a day more than adequate.

Enjoy your last week!

Day 22

Here Before

Tuesday is ballet day; Olivia loves ballet and I love to watch. I grab a highchair and put Stanley into it. At just over ten months, a steady stream of snacks is essential for him. Olivia kisses her baby brother; he grabs at her nose and they both giggle.

Olivia leans in, "Love you, Mum."

"Love you, Liv."

She skips off to the ballet studio. I pop a rice cake into Stanley's pudgy hand and one on his tray; that should buy me five minutes. I gaze through the window at Olivia. She is so graceful and listens intently to her teacher. I am so proud of her. The viewing room is filled with parents, mostly on laptops, paying no attention to the ballet. I try not to judge but they are missing out. I'm sure they would say I don't understand because I don't work, but sometimes everything else can wait.

A flustered lady sits at the table closest to ours and takes out her laptop. She has clearly come straight from work and she's hurried her two daughters in for their lesson. I think I've seen her here before. Stanley is blowing raspberries, shouting and giggling. He is waving a spoon and no amount of distraction will stop him staring at her. She turns and I am pleasantly surprised to find her face is warm and welcoming.

"Hello, baba," she says, and gives him a wave. He is delighted and continues his happy mixture of eating and babbling. She turns every few minutes, saying hello, blowing raspberries and playing peekaboo. I smile but we don't talk. I watch Olivia dance and she waves at me every time she has a break. I mime clapping and give her a thumbs up. She is so talented. I turn to give Stanley another snack and find the woman from the table is standing right next to him, and he is holding onto her finger.

"Hi," I say, trying not to sound startled. She strokes the side of his cheek and does not take her eyes off him.

"Isn't he funny?"

I'm not entirely sure what she means. "He is a bit noisy, sorry."

"No, I mean, he's not new, is he? He's been here before."

That doesn't clear things up, but I don't want to be rude. "No, he's not new, we come every week."

She has not stopped staring at Stanley, smiling and talking under her breath to him. She turns to me but there is no eye contact.

"He's lovely." She goes back to her seat and doesn't look over again, and I feed Stanley a yoghurt.

Lessons are over; her girls come out and the three of them leave before Olivia even emerges. She is full of energy and she hugs us both before we make our way to the car. Olivia munches crisps and apple juice on the way home and looks dreamily out of the window.

"Fish fingers?"

"That's perfect, Mum, thanks." She is such a good girl. David is working away tonight, and I hate to cook. Stanley is napping and I think briefly of the woman; odd, definitely odd. I might ask Olivia about her daughters tomorrow.

I sort tea while Olivia grabs a shower. I never need to check on my independent and meticulous eight-year-old. Stanley is happily sitting on his play mat, bashing building blocks together and giggling. Olivia comes bounding in, all wrapped up in her fluffy baby-blue dressing gown, her golden hair beautifully brushed. She stops and pulls silly faces at Stanley on the way past and sits at the table with her sequinned notebook and beautifully organised pencil case. We eat our fish finger feast and I treat us to a few squares of milk chocolate for finishing all our peas.

"Fifteen more minutes drawing, Liv, while I bath Stanley, then bedtime for all of us."

I bath Stanley and hear Olivia heading to her bedroom to read. Stanley and I settle down for a feed on the rocking chair in his room and then I place him gently in his cot. He is exhausted and will be asleep by the time I'm halfway through Olivia's story. I tiptoe next door, but Olivia isn't there, and she's not in the bathroom either. I go downstairs, where she is back at the table.

"Sorry, Mum, I just really needed to finish off this last bit to give to Eva at school tomorrow."

"That's OK, sweetheart, but next time..."

She is engrossed in her writing, so I give her a big hug.

"Bedtime, my love." She nods reluctantly, and we head upstairs. I grab Stanley's monitor and switch it on, although he is already silent. I am so lucky, he is such a good baby. I read Olivia's story and let her have some reading time of her own.

"Fifteen minutes then lights out, it's school tomorrow."

"Night, Mum."

"Night, Liv, love you."

I sneak downstairs and pour myself a good-sized gin and tonic. I love David very much, but Tuesday nights are my guilty pleasure; I snuggle under the covers in our bed, grab my book and sip my gin. Stanley will wake around 4am for a feed so after two chapters, I finish my drink and turn out the light. I feel nervous when David works away, and the exhaustion and gin help me drift off.

Stanley's cry through the monitor wakes me. I check my phone and it's only 11.30pm - that's not like him. He cries a few times and then stops, so I lie back down and pull the covers around me. His monitor is making a weird noise, almost like static from a TV. I hold it to my ear, then decide I'll go and check on him. I open his door and wait for my eyes to adjust, but it takes less than a second for me to realise that he is not in his cot. My body prickles with fear and dread. I see the shape in the rocking chair; she is holding him, gently stroking his hair, and making a shushing sound. The tree mural on his wall looks grotesque and frightening in the dark, growing out of the top of her head like snakes. I can't speak. What if she hurts him? I sit on the floor, tuck my knees to my chest and cry, watching her rock back and forth. She has not looked at me.

"Please." It's all that comes out through my sobs. She turns and puts a finger to her mouth to quieten me.

She whispers, "I couldn't leave him here with you."

A new wave of fear hits me. "Please, just give him to me, just leave, please." I slowly get on my knees and lean towards them, but she recoils sharply and holds Stanley tightly to her chest. He starts to protest, and she rocks him gently.

Her whisper becomes a hiss. "He was mine. My Jamie." For the first time, she looks directly at me, her eyes wild and wide.

"I knew he'd come back to me." She's obviously deranged but I need to make her see sense somehow. I know she won't give him back, and I think I am going to have to take him. As if sensing my intention, she shows me a small, silver knife in her other hand.

"He will always come back for me. He can be mine in the next life if you don't let us go." She stands up and walks past me, holding my baby. I can't let her go, she'll hurt him anyway. I follow her and she holds the knife close to his cheek. He is wriggling but not yet awake. My heart is racing, and I feel out of control. She has me and she knows it. I cannot risk his life and I have absolutely no idea what to do.

She goes to open the front door. "If you take a step outside, I will kill us both." I want to scream, I want to grab Stanley, I want to kill her, but I watch her open the door, helpless. She has a knife and my baby, I have nothing. I stand there, shaking inside and choking on my tears. I watch her walk down the path, but suddenly something takes over and I let out a shriek and lunge out of my door towards her. She turns and I am knocked off my feet, winded and searching for breath, clambering and scraping at the ground, trying to get to Stanley. I feel hands grab my shoulders, and I shake and lash out and scream with every fibre of my being.

"Calm down, it's OK." It's a man's voice and they aren't her hands on my shoulders; a police officer is holding me. That woman is on the ground, staring straight at me, eyes unblinking. I see the knife sticking out of the side of her neck and her head is surrounded by blood. I hear Stanley crying; he is being brought towards me by another police officer. I see splashes of blood on him, but he is perfectly fine otherwise. I am helped to my feet with Stanley in my arms.

"Your daughter called us, she's in your bedroom."

I look again to the horrific sight of the dead woman on my drive, and the police officer senses my fear.

"She did it herself. You're safe. Go be with your family."

I run upstairs with Stanley in my arms to Olivia, who is crying and clearly terrified.

"You saved us, you saved us both." I kiss and embrace her, and I am overcome with love for both of them. I know I will need to deal with the horror downstairs and the effects it may have on all of us, but for now, everything else can wait.

Day 23

Big News

If someone had told me that one day everyone over the age of forty would suddenly drop dead, I would have thought it was the craziest thing I had ever heard. But, eighteen months on and the oldest person in the world is forty-one. I was forty last month.

It started with a noise, like a rumble inside your ears. I close my eyes and make the noise; I'm getting good at it. I've no idea how it actually sounded. Four days the strongest lasted, I rumble again, I like that noise, it can't have been so bad. It wasn't dramatic; they just didn't wake up.

I don't know why it happened. To be honest, I'm not bothered. For four days it was an apocalyptic shit show, but then it was done. Why seems unimportant somehow. I made it and I don't want to take my brain back there. There is enough food and stuff now for twice as many people. There was no grief, I think because it affected everyone the same. You can only suffer if someone else is not, but we all were, or maybe we weren't. I rumble my ears. Can adults even be orphans?

My phone vibrates with a message. "Looking forward to tonight. I'll be there as close to eight as poss, enjoy xx." I smile; I'll answer later.

Life is easy. A late breakfast in front of the TV. I could sit here in my underwear all day if I wish, my bills are taken care of, I've no one to look after and no one to tell me what I should and shouldn't do. I'll go for jog if I can be bothered, then a long shower before dinner and drinks later. I've got big news, today is going to be a good day.

Survivors are mostly better off than they were, most people are happier, but they can't say it, I wish somebody would. It's like the party you have when your parents go on holiday. I talked to my therapist about it (they are coining it in by the way) and he said something about survivors' guilt. I don't buy it.

I check the news and immediately wish I hadn't. I had better get dressed, I am sure this will not be pretty either way, but I'd rather wait and see on my own terms. My phone vibrates again. "Have you seen the news? I'm coming home early, see you soon xx." Today will not be a good day, my growing baby is no longer good news, this is so irritating. I can't be here when Jack gets home from work, he won't realise I'm in trouble. When you lie about your age, you don't consider a fucking apocalypse. I grab my coat and boots. Bad choice, I need to look young and opt for hoody and trainers instead. I put my hair in a low ponytail and contemplate pigtails but that may be overkill. I can easily pass for under thirty-five.

The newsreader is interviewing someone outside a hospital, and the headline at the bottom tells me all I need to know. The virus is back.

"Do we know how many have died or how many are ill?"

"According to a source, five people are dead, and more are ill, but this is unconfirmed at present."

"Are we sure this is a recurrence of the same virus?"

I turn it off. What else could it be? I go out immediately. If the government's plan is to wait for four days and then scoop up bodies, that doesn't work for me. Why didn't I give a shit when this was happening to everyone else? There will be less of us this time, there can't be too many people who have turned forty in the last eighteen months. Maybe we can all go on life support until it's over. I can't get sick anyway; at barely three months pregnant, saving my baby most definitely involves saving myself.

I walk quickly and go into a half-empty coffee shop, but it's a bit grim.

I don't recognise anyone and go and sit in a quiet booth with my green tea.

"OK, Google, time to save my life." I start simple and see if anyone did in fact work out how to survive this shit. Maybe someone has it all figured out and there's a handy tablet that I just have to pick up. Unsurprisingly, no. Instead there is a wealth of mostly batshit-crazy nonsense. However, I am not currently in a position to judge and I am certainly not above dancing naked in the blood of chickens if it will get me out of this. There's no credible evidence of survival; there is the odd person who turned out to be younger than they thought, but how the fuck does that happen? The best thing I can find is something to do with sound frequencies. I don't understand the science at all, which is hopeful. On the homepage, the author of the website has a list of instructions for survival. I'm quickly running out of time and options.

1. Do not speak to anyone, including yourself.

2. Do not watch any live TV or listen to live radio.

3. Do not use the telephone.

4. Expose your ears to constant sound; pre-recorded TV or music, must be pre-2018,

DO NOT let it stop.

5. Lie down and sleep as much as possible.

6. Do all the above for five days.

Clearly this is stupid, but I have nothing to lose and I am too scared to go home. I pay and go to Mum's old house. Dad died a couple of years earlier. I hate that all this shit happened just as Mum was recovering, I know Mum had been found in the house curled up on the sofa in the living room. I don't ever think about it.

I gather up all the DVDs I can find, leaving a few of Dad's frankly unwatchable westerns but keeping Mum's legs, bums and tums; I've got five bloody days to fill. I find my dad's old CD player and my parents' stack of CDs; a mixture of slushy ballads and 70s rock. This is so unfair. I set their bell alarm clock to go off every two hours in case I drop off, then turn my phone off and take the battery out. I'm quite sure I have an inflated sense of my own importance here, but I'm still not taking any chances. The hours pass quickly, I eat too much, and I watch my favourite DVDs too early. After 12 hours I want to smash the alarm clock and it's going to ring another 48 times. I keep checking for a rumble in my ears, but there's nothing yet and with every hour I get more hopeful. I stay as still as possible and only leave the bed when I must; it's perfect apocalypse survival behaviour.

I worry about Jack. I hope he will have figured out what has happened. I couldn't leave a note for him, but I do worry he won't forgive me if I survive. I think of Mum and Dad, and I haven't allowed myself to do that in ages; too painful in a way, but it's also nice. Hours pass. I really miss my phone. I put my head under the covers and hide. I have a weirdest DVD-and-song-combination competition and it's a toss-up between *Bambi* and Led Zeppelin or *The Exorcist* and Bette Midler. I think I'll leave *The Shining* for another day. Three days in and I consider turning my phone on. There has been no rumble, and I'm smelly and concerned I'm losing it a bit.

"The other option is death, you fucking idiot." The rules! Shit. Imagine if I died because I shouted at myself, the irony. The bell rings for the 59th time. I spend half that time deciding whether I have got the numbers right and is it 60, or 59, or maybe even 61. I don't care anymore; in 17 minutes I can turn my phone on.

My phone buzzes. There are an alarming number of messages and voicemails. I open my news app; I need to know how bad it is. The headline is not exactly what I was expecting, something about the biggest iceberg in Antarctica. What the hell has been going on? I scroll and eventually find it; some factually incorrect information leaked by someone in the hospital and blown out of proportion. You could not make this shit up. I feel like the world's biggest idiot, but who cares, I am not dead or dying. I jump up and down on the bed.

I remember Jack hasn't got a clue where I am and sit down to tackle my messages. At least a dozen from Jack, all asking where I am and getting more frantic. Nothing for the last two days though. Four voicemails.

"Laura, give me a call, please, I'm at yours, love you, bye."

"Laura, I'm getting a bit worried now. You didn't answer my other messages and the ones I'm sending now aren't getting through. Just let me know you're OK, love you, bye."

"Laura, please, I don't know what's happening. If you're mad at me or something is wrong... Look, a one-word message will do, please."

I feel terrible. He sounds so worried, but hopefully he will understand, and be delighted about the baby. The last one is a voice I don't immediately recognise.

"Laura, I don't know whether you'll get this or not..."

It's Nate, Jack's brother. Why would Nate call me?

"... Jack's been arrested. They think he's kidnapped or murdered you or something. Please, just get in touch with someone, anyone."

His voice cracks and the phone cuts off.

Day 24

In Time

He's snoring as usual and it takes me several shakes to wake him.

"I can hear a noise!" I tell him.

"What? What do you..."

"Downstairs, in the kitchen. Can you go and check?"

He sighs and starts to slowly get out of bed.

"There! You must have heard it this time."

He grabs our big, heavy torch and heads downstairs. My heart is pounding, but I can't hear anything that sounds worrying and, after five minutes, I hear his footsteps coming back upstairs.

"It's just Anaya."

"Anaya? What's she doing? Where's Asha?"

"In her room, I assume. She's sat at the kitchen table, half asleep. She wants you, must be a women's thing." He uses this every time since she became a teenager.

"That's such a shit excuse, Mohit."

"Anne, she wants you. Just go and check she's OK, she's acting odd."

I tiptoe downstairs after checking on Asha. Anaya is sitting at the kitchen table, her back to me and her shoulders hunched over.

"Anaya?" She ignores me, I sit with her and hold her hand. If her eyes were closed, I would be certain she is asleep. She looks through me and speaks in a monotone voice.

"It will burn."

I don't want to shock or scare her. "Anaya, are you OK?"

I don't think she hears me, and she continues with the same voice. "You won't get out." Tears fall from her face onto the kitchen table. She's scaring me now, and I shake her shoulders.

"Anaya, wake up, Anaya."

She wakes from her trance and focuses on my face. "Mum?"

She looks around and clearly has no recollection of what just happened. "Why are we in the kitchen?"

"You were just sleep walking, sweetheart. Don't worry about it, let's just get you to bed."

She nods and as we hug, I can feel her shaking.

Mohit is snoring again but manages, "she OK?" as I noisily get back into bed.

"She's fine, just sleepwalking. Hopefully, it's not something that will happen again." He's asleep before I finish my sentence.

Everyone is fine the next morning. Anaya and Asha get up and off to school without a hitch and nobody mentions last night's events. I'm probably being overanxious, but I can't shake my sense of unease over what she said.

The next night, I hear a noise, a different noise. I think someone is at the front door. Mohit is sleeping and I grab the torch. I am shaking with fear, but I want to do this on my own. From the top of the stairs, I can see that our front door is open. Anaya stands on the doorstep with bare feet and only her nightgown. She must be freezing.

I run and wrap my dressing gown around her, but she doesn't respond and her eyes are absent, just as they were last night.

"They won't get there in time." That monotone voice again. I know I should wake her and bring her in to the warmth.

"Anaya, who won't get there in time?"

She turns and walks back inside and starts to walk slowly upstairs in her dreamlike state. She stops halfway up the stairs and turns her head to face the wall. In the darkness, I can see her profile but not her eyes.

"You'll die." She faces front again and keeps walking. I stand frozen until I hear her bedroom door close. I consider shaking Mohit awake. I need him. I'm terrified Anaya is having some sort of breakdown, or maybe it's just nightmares or even hormones. I don't know what to do but I do know he won't be any use in the middle of the night. I lie awake, alone and worrying until I drift off.

"Morning, Anaya." She is at the breakfast table alone. "You're up and ready early. Everything OK?"

"Fine, Mum. I woke up really hungry and cold, so I had a hot shower and some toast. Want some?" She smiles and holds a piece out to me.

"Do you remember last night?"

"What do you mean?"

"You were sleepwalking. I found you at the front door."

"What? Are you for real?" She looks genuinely taken aback. "Mum, that's like really scary."

"I'm sure it's just a one-off thing. Has anything changed? Is anything bothering you?"

"No, everything's fine. Well, except Asha but, you know..."

I'm relieved. Bickering between sisters is nothing new and she seems genuine that nothing else is wrong.

I wake the next night and know the front door is open before I leave my room. Terror consumes me when she isn't in the doorway. I see her silhouette, barefoot on the stony driveway. She is a frightening sight, with a kitchen knife in one hand and a hammer in the other, rain pouring down on her. What is happening to my beautiful girl? Her eyes are closed, eyelids fluttering, and she is breathing as though she has just finished sprinting. She holds out her weapons to me as though in surrender and walks carefully back inside. I get into my car and push the knife and hammer under the passenger seat. I push my palms into my eyes. I would give anything for this to go away. I feel helpless and scared for Anaya. I know I can't fix this on my own, but I'm terrified of what might happen to her if I ask for help. Still, I know I have to protect my child, even if that means protecting her from herself.

I explain to Mohit the next morning at breakfast, leaving out the disturbing details. "I'm going to make a doctor's appointment for Anaya. She's sleepwalking every night and I'm worried she'll fall down the stairs."

"Doctor? She probably just needs to get off her phone."

He can be so dismissive, but I'm fearful of how he'd react if I told him everything.

"You're probably right, but I'd rather be safe than sorry. Why don't we let her sleep in while we all go to the shops? We could surprise her with a nice brunch or something?"

He shrugs, which knowing Mohit is as enthusiastic as he'll get.

"Asha, come and get in the car. We need to go and get some shopping."

"Where's Anaya?"

"She's sleeping. We'll leave a note for her and see her when we get back."

"That's so unfair!"

She's got a point, but she soon cheers up with the promise of cake.

Mohit is a terrible driver but insists on driving. I've given up arguing about it. The traffic is terrible, and my thoughts turn to Anaya. At least she doesn't know about what's been happening. I'm glad she's not scared but

I'm petrified about what might happen next. I'm suddenly jolted out of my daydream as I'm thrown violently forward. There is a sharp, terrible pain in my chest, and I can taste blood. I can feel glass all around me and I can see Mohit unconscious and slumped over the wheel. A lorry has hit us from behind and we have been squashed into the car in front.

I turn and Asha is behind me. She is squashed up against the seat and thankfully doesn't seem hurt. She is clearly in shock, staring at me with wide, terrified eyes.

"It's OK, Asha, everything is going to be fine. I'll get us out." She nods and I recognise the faint smell of smoke. I know we have to get out fast. I can't undo our seatbelts; the clasps are buried and I can barely move. I scrabble around by my feet and cut my hand on the blade of the knife. I hear Anaya's voice in my head. "You'll die." I am on autopilot. I cut my seatbelt and then Mohit's, and I smash my side window and force the door with the hammer. I reach back for Asha but her door is open and she is standing on the pavement. She looks so small and confused, and I scoop her up and carry her away before dragging Mohit out of the car. I fall, sobbing, as our car sets on fire. We are alive, and Anaya saved us.

The rest of the day is a blur. Asha doesn't have a scratch on her, but Mohit has a minor head injury and has to stay in hospital for a couple of days. I have a couple of bruised ribs and some cuts and bruises, but I am grateful to be back home with my girls. I can tell by how shocked and tearful Anaya is that she has no memory or understanding of any of this. I have no explanations that don't sound crazy, but I know my daughter saved us, that her love for us did this somehow. I hope she'll sleep soundly now.

"Mum! Mum!" I hear Anaya shout from her room. I jump out of bed and run to her. Asha is stood at the foot of Anaya's bed, and Anaya is huddled against the wall away from her.

"Mum, get her out of here."

"Asha, what are you doing in here, sweetheart?" My heart sinks as I recognise her trance-like state. She looks through me and walks slowly back to her own room.

I throw my arms around Anaya. "She's just sleepwalking, darling, her sleep will be messed up because of the crash. We've all had a hard day."

Anaya nods and seems much calmer.

I ask her, "Did Asha say anything to you?"

"Yes," Anaya says. "It was weird though. She said, 'Why did you fix it?'"

Day 25

The Girl in the Shop

I've been standing outside long enough. I don't know what I am so afraid of. I can just look around; people do that all the time. I'm afraid of letting myself hope again. As I walk through the door, the first thing I see is an enormous cross-stitch panda framed on the wall. I stop and stare and take it all in. It's so beautiful and exquisitely crafted that it looks like a photograph. The young lady behind the counter catches me staring and smiles warmly at me. She has a laptop behind the counter, and she has an art student vibe.

"I absolutely adore the panda," I say to her, and I really mean it. I am completely in love with him. He looks strong and brave and he makes me feel good inside.

"Thank you." Her pale skin blushes slightly, although she doesn't appear shy at all.

"You did this?" I am so impressed; it is magnificent, and I understand the level of dedication that something like that would take.

"It took me two years. I love him, but I keep him here for the children who come in and hopefully they'll want to try some cross-stitch too. But yours is the best reaction I've had so far!" She giggles and I stare at the panda some more.

"I really do love him." I've almost forgotten why I came into the craft store in the first place, but I'm glad of the distraction as I feel much less nervous. "Sorry, I am looking for some oil paints, brushes and some linen canvas."

She wanders over to the paints. "Any specific colours?"

I nod. "A basic starter set." I join her and start picking out colours.

She watches my choices. "You're clearly not a new starter."

I meet her eye. "No, just making a new start." I tell her about my situation. I gloss over a lot of the detail but it's the most open I think I've ever been with a stranger. There's something about the environment in here that makes me feel less stiff and anxious. I am soaking in the creativity and all the beautiful possibilities and things that could be made this is where I am meant to be, surrounded by things like this.

"I've realised that the biggest mistake I have made in all of this is staying in a good job that isn't right for me because it feels like the right thing to do." I have no idea why I am telling her all of this, and I'm sure she wishes I would just buy the paint and piss off, but she seems to understand.

"And today is your first step towards correcting that mistake?"

"Sort of. I've had a funny couple of days, and I feel different. What I really want is to be happy and I need to make some big changes to get there. I'm worried if I don't keep the momentum of the last couple of days, then I might wake up afraid again tomorrow. Do you know what I mean?" I look her in the eye again, mostly to see if she's either bored or thinks I've lost it. Thankfully, it appears to be neither. She's looking thoughtful and goes to get her laptop. On the screen is a beautiful floral pattern that's clearly a work in progress but it is unique and mesmerising.

"I'm an artist, too." She smiles at her work and then at me. "I'm a fabric designer for women's clothing."

I am thrilled for her. "That's incredible, absolutely amazing!" I think I am overdoing it but I'm so impressed by her talent and the fact she has been able to find work. "Who do you design for?"

"Nobody, yet." She stands up tall and pulls her shoulders back. "But that doesn't mean I am not a fabric designer, the same way that you are still a portrait artist, no matter where you work."

Her words lift me and fill me with excitement. She is right, I am standing in my own way. I have been so afraid of failure that I haven't even tried.

"Thank you. You don't know how much I needed to hear that." We head back to the paints and finish choosing. I pick a small selection of paint brushes. I prefer to paint with larger brushes and they have exactly what I am looking for. I have everything I need for a basic portrait. I have the solvents I like to use at home, and I choose one large and one small linen canvas.

"Will you paint yourself?"

"No, I don't like to paint myself." Lewis won't be home until late tonight. "I guess I'll just look through some old photos on my computer and paint from one of those." It all feels a bit less exciting now somehow. For me, painting is all about feeling and I love to have someone sit for me, even if only briefly. I need a sense of who they are in that moment to make a painting come to life.

She nods. "Can I borrow your phone?" She takes a picture of herself. It's fantastic. There's a look in her eyes that captures everything about our meeting and the magnificent panda is behind her head, so it's simply perfect. I can see the painting coming to life, my head is swimming and I can't wait to get home and get started.

She hands me a business card. "Send me a picture of your painting before you go to bed. It doesn't have to be finished; I'd just like to see it. In the evenings I cross-stitch and that leaves my head open for pattern ideas for the next day."

"Of course! I can't thank you enough." I feel like hugging her. I really can't thank her enough and I leave her to her designing and head home smiling.

I lay out all my art supplies on the kitchen table, then choose the big canvas and write on the back in pencil, "The girl in the shop". I realise I don't know her name, and I don't think I told her mine either.

According to her business card, her name is Joanna Jonnsen. There are a couple of key things missing that I hadn't thought about in my haste, but I can't let that stop me. I have avoided painting or even thinking about painting for far too long and I shudder at the thought of going back to that again. So I make do, using the chair from my dressing table as an easel and an old photo frame as a pallet. I throw my stiff work clothes onto the floor and get comfortable; I tie my hair up in a messy bun and stare at myself in the mirror. The reflection looking back at me is happy and excited and that is exactly how I feel. I realise this is exactly how I should be feeling about work and I only wish this were the uniform I could wear to work every day. I position the chair and canvas at the end of one of the kitchen benches and set out my paints, makeshift pallet and solvent, and crack open a window. I breathe deeply; it feels like a new beginning.

Painting from a tiny picture on my phone is not ideal but today is about beginning, not perfection. It all comes back to me so easily and feels completely natural. Within thirty minutes I have a bold, dark and messy outline of Joanna and the panda. I step back and feel proud. There is a likeness of her already; she looks alive. I want to keep my promise to Joanna so I focus in on her face, leaving the panda for tomorrow. I add layers of paint, building her face up and adding structure, then I add intensity to her eyes and depth to her hair. I give her emotion and warmth, and give life to the knowing smile on her face. You don't paint a portrait; you feel it and always leave something of yourself behind. I want her to feel how she's helped me today, just from looking at the picture.

I feel exhausted and I know that I've hit my limit for today. I look flushed and elated, like I've just stepped off a rollercoaster or been on a fabulous first date. I clean myself up and get into my pyjamas, and then I hear Lewis come through the door. I tiptoe through to the kitchen and he is there staring at my painting.

"Samantha." His voice is breathy, he sounds astonished. "Did you do this?"

I feel weirdly embarrassed but manage a nod.

He shakes his head. I can see he is amazed. "It's beautiful, just incredibly beautiful."

Tears prick my eyes and he runs over and envelopes me in a warm and welcome hug.

"You are so incredibly talented, Samantha. I can't believe I didn't know this about you. You should be sharing this with the world, it's completely amazing."

I bury myself in his chest and feel more whole than I have in a long time. We curl up on the sofa with a bottle of wine and a hastily prepared dinner. I remember my promise and send Joanna a photo of the painting.

She responds immediately. "I love it, you have a special talent x."

I reply, "Thank you (for everything) x."

"Remember, creativity takes courage and things won't change if you don't change them yourself. Believe in yourself."

Sitting here in Lewis's arms and reading Joanna's messages, I believe in myself more than I ever have, and I know this time I won't give up.

Day 26

Escape

My bowl of half-eaten cereal crashes to the floor. It's been fifteen years. She looks dirty and scared but I can't find any words. She must be nineteen now.

"Kieran?" Her voice is the same, her eyes are the same and she remembers my name, even though she hasn't seen me since I was a scruffy eight-year-old boy.

"Sophie." I don't ask it as a question. I've always known she was alive. She falls into my arms and I can feel her bones poking into me. I carry her to the living room as she weeps silently, soaking the shoulder of my T-shirt. She doesn't let go of me. I wish Mum were here, because I don't know what to do and I can't handle the emotions bouncing around in my brain.

"Sophie, I'm so sorry... how?" Tears sting my eyes. I don't want her to answer, I don't want to hear what has happened to her. I have only made it through the last fifteen years by refusing to believe any of the horrific things I know she could have been subjected to.

Her voice is barely a whisper. "I escaped, Kieran, I finally escaped." She breaks down and cries so violently I worry her tiny bones may shatter.

I hold her face in my hands. "You're safe now, Soph, I won't let anything bad happen to you again. We're going to call Mum and then the police. Everything will be OK, I promise." I hug her tightly; I have no idea how

I'm going to tell Mum and, at that moment, I realise Sophie doesn't know that Dad is dead either.

I call Mum and tell her to come home urgently. I can't tell her over the phone. I'll wait until Mum is here before calling the police. I don't want her to come home to find a police car outside. Sophie seems sleepy and she sips the tea I made for her. I'm scared to ask any questions, but I feel guilty and uncaring in the silence.

"Do you still live here with Mum and Dad?"

I was hoping I wouldn't have to be the one to tell her. Dad and Soph were so close and I've always believed he would still be alive if Sophie hadn't gone missing.

"I moved in when Dad died just over a year ago."

She doesn't look surprised but suddenly bursts into tears, and shrieks through her sobs. It's quite a performance. "Dad, oh no, Dad! What happened, Kieran?"

Her behaviour is odd, and I stop myself from staring and remind myself of what she's been through. I'm sure my behaviour would be odd, too. Still, there's something, but I'm sure she'll tell me when she's ready.

"He had a stroke, a big one. He didn't even make it to hospital. Hit us like a ton of bricks. I didn't think Mum would cope after losing you, too, so I moved in."

I see something in her eyes just for a second, and then it disappears. A nervous feeling creeps over me and I realise what is bothering me. She looks like Sophie, but there's something different, something unusual.

Mum bursts through the door, "Kieran, what the bloody hell is..."

She stops and stares at Sophie. She leans against the door for support but slides to the floor anyway. All the colour has drained from her face and she looks like she has seen a ghost.

Sophie springs out of her chair and runs to her. "I'm home, Mum, I'm home." Mum doesn't speak and they embrace and cry in a tangled heap on the floor. "I escaped, Mum, I'm back home."

Mum looks as white as a sheet; she is shaking her head and her mouth is gaping. I watch them as they help each other up and sit together on the sofa. Mum looks petrified and Sophie is grinning and crying. I can't look. I go to make tea.

We sip tea and I feel like I'm in a weird parallel universe. Everything has changed dramatically in less than two hours, but why is nobody saying anything?

"Should I call the police?" I offer.

"Sophie and I will call them together after we've finished tea." Sophie and Mum exchange a look that I don't understand, and hug each other. There's something bubbling underneath, and I'm clearly being kept away from it.

"I want you to go to the shops, Kieran. Here's a list of things for Sophie."

"But..."

"No, it's not for you to hear the details. Sophie is home now, and we are going to focus on making her happy and catching up on all the years we have lost." Another look and another hug. I think I should get out of here before I say something stupid.

I get everything Mum asked for. I have been deliberately sent to as many shops as possible, but I still manage it in just over an hour. Sophie is all cleaned up, and she looks so much better, even in my old jogging bottoms and T-shirt. I get a weird monologue from Mum, that the police have been, Sophie has told them where her kidnapper is, it's all sorted and we aren't to mention it again, thank you very much. Sophie was being held in a basement, she hasn't been hurt or abused in any way, and no questions from you, thank you, Kieran.

I should feel relieved, but I feel irritated and pushed out. If Dad were here, he wouldn't be putting up with this. Every question I have asked has been shot down. Why is her hair nicely cut? How does she know how everything works? Maybe I'm just being paranoid, but a nineteen-year-old girl being held captive in a basement probably didn't have a tablet or a phone, so how is she sitting here, using them like... like nothing happened. Mum is getting irritated with me. I love her more than anything, but she's controlling and behaves like a two-year-old if you don't do everything her way. She's a very weird adult.

"Kieran, why can't you just be grateful that your sister's back?"

"I am, it's just..."

Mum puts her hand over mine. "You know everything you need to know. She doesn't want to hurt you, she wants you to see her as your sister, not as a victim. She can't move on otherwise." I can see she is pleading with me to leave it alone, and maybe she's right, maybe Sophie is just protecting me. I'd probably do the same with her. But still, one day is awfully quick to be talking about moving on, isn't it?

"Sorry, Mum, it's just all a bit much, you know? I'm sorry."

She hugs me and I can see she's glad I'm back with the programme.

"I think I'll head out for a run," I say, "clear my head a bit."

I get one of her weird hugs. I don't know how to explain it. She's a good person, she's caring and kind and totally selfless, but nothing seems quite real, almost as if there's a fear of something that drives everything and no reaction is genuine. Whatever the reason, I know it must be hard for her so I hug her back, a genuine hug.

I run around the corner and crouch behind our back-garden fence. In ten minutes, I'll sneak through the back door. They won't hear me. I don't actually care what has been going on, but I know they are in on something together, something that they'll never tell me. I can only just hear them from the kitchen - do I risk it? I creep further and hide just outside the living room door. Mum is talking.

"... maybe, but what have you told Bob and Rosa?"

"That I'm coming back here. I've never been happy there, Mum. I understand why you did it, there's no hard feelings, I just want to be home. I'm all grown up now, things are different."

Mum sounds teary. "I want you to be home, too, Sophie, but I can see Kieran knows something. I don't know why we told him what we did."

"Then just tell him, I'm sure..."

I hear Mum's voice harden. "No. Never. I've ruined things with you, I can't face that with Kieran."

"Then what, you send me away like an inconvenience again?"

"You know that's not what happened, Sophie, you know why we did it. I appreciate it must have been terrible for you, but you were not an inconvenience. Don't say that."

I've heard enough, I get the gist. What I want most in the world is for Mum to be happy and my sister to be safe, and I have that. I go on the run I promised them and come back with a much clearer head.

Sophie flings her arms around my neck when I come in and immediately regrets it. "Yuck, you are so sweaty!"

"I have been running, you twit!" She laughs. That's the strongest word I could use, as in my mind she's still four. Things feel much closer to normal than ever, I think.

Sophie is very excitable this evening. She must be on such a roller coaster of emotions. I've stopped asking questions and they both seem relieved. Sophie has planned our evening for us.

"I don't want to dwell on the past anymore, I want tonight to be a proper celebration, so I've ordered us a takeaway. Sorry, Mum, I had to use your money, I don't own anything yet! There's a movie starting after the news. Let's have a nice family evening and get to know each other again?"

Mum looks so happy, and I'm happy for her. I go to change the channel; there's a horrible news story about a couple being butchered in their home. It's going to take me some time to get used to my baby sister being an adult. But before I use the remote, Mum stands, shrieking and pointing at the TV.

"Bob and Rosa! Bob... and... Rosa! What the..."

Sophie is laughing, cackling and throwing her head back. She jumps and claps like a child.

"I killed them, I killed them! Tra-la-la!"

Mum is shaking and holding her chest.

"Oh, stop faking it, Mum, or do us all a favour and drop dead quickly." This Sophie is pure evil, but at least this time I know it's her, it's real. Mum is barely audible.

"You monster, how could you do that to..."

Sophie is still chaotic and bouncing around the room. I need to call the police before this gets any worse.

"Don't fucking move, Kieran." She catches me and I sit down.

I look at Mum, swaying and sobbing.

"I had to send her away, Kieran, she was always like this and we didn't know what to do, we thought she would hurt you." I see a horrible realisation in her eyes, a feeling of responsibility for the deaths being described on the TV. "Oh God, Bob and Rosa, you evil, evil child!"

Sophie stands and walks until her face is inches from Mum's. "You made me like this, you, Mother! It's you that's evil, don't you ever forget that."

I move to grab Mum.

"Sit. The. Fuck. Down. Kieran. I will kill her if you don't."

I sit. There is evidence of what she is capable of right in front of me.

Sophie grabs my mother's cheeks and squeezes hard. "Death is too good for you, Mother dear. Hopefully the guilt will get you sooner rather than later, but for now, I'm happy to know that you are suffering. I killed Bob and Rosa because of you, maybe even for you."

She grins and waves as she leaves, pausing only briefly to blow me a kiss. I have no idea what to feel. Mum is sobbing and heaving as though she may vomit.

"Kieran... I..." She can't finish because there are no words for what has just happened. Nothing will ever make this right for her ever again, but I know one thing - secrets and lies are not going to fix this. They have only made it worse, and then much worse.

"Mum, I'm calling the police."

She shakes her head furiously, but she's getting no choice. Every action has consequences and we will all have to take what comes.

Day 27

Be Good

I wake up coughing. My throat is raw; I can taste blood and there are lumps of something in my mouth. I roll onto my side and spit out what I can. One of my eyes opens easily, the other feels open but I can't see. I'm scared to touch my face. I don't know what I might find, and if there's no eye to find I'd rather not know just yet. I'm on a hard floor and the room is dark, but I can start to make out some shadows. I think I'm in a bedroom and I know I haven't been here before. The last thing I remember is being in the taxi with Marvin. Marvin... If I'm here, then where is my husband? I'm almost certain I'm alone and I don't want whoever put me here to come back.

"Marvin," I whisper. There's no answer. I don't know whether to be relieved or not. I rub my jaw, and it's painful to touch. The stubble on my face is long so I think I've been out at least a couple of days. I reach to gently check my eye and realise it is fine, and my head is partially covered with a hood. I'm fully clothed but my suit jacket, tie, shoes and socks are missing.

Suddenly the door opens and a man with his face covered walks in. He turns on the lights and I'm temporarily blinded. I squint and scramble my way into the corner. I'm in someone's office, and there's something familiar about him but I can't place it. He has a bag of takeaway food and a drink. He puts it on the table and motions for me to sit and eat. I'm terrified but I have to do something. I'd bolt for the door, but he'd get there first and who knows what he'd do to me.

"Where's Marvin?" He doesn't answer, he turns and walks towards the door. I scramble to my feet.

"Please, who are you, what is... Why do you have..." I can't form a coherent question. He ignores me again and moves closer to the door. My fear turns to rage and I start screaming and waving my arms.

"Where the fuck is Marvin? Why the fuck am I here, who the fuck are -" He runs over to me and pulls the hood down over my head so tightly that I can't breathe. He's going to kill me; he's probably already killed Marvin. I feel his breath through the cloth next to my ear.

"You've got forty-eight hours. Be good and nothing will happen to you. Ask me another question and next time I won't let go of this hood until you've stopped breathing."

I think I'm going to pass out.

"Nod your head to let me know you understand."

I do as he says.

"Good, now I'm going to get up and leave and, if you make any move, I will kill you immediately, believe me."

I do believe him.

"There are cameras in this room, and I will be watching. If you make any attempt to escape, try to open any window or the door, I will come straight back and I will kill you. There are no second chances, do you understand?"

I nod.

"Good, forty-eight hours, do as I say, eat the food and don't ask any questions."

He rips the hood off, and I sit in silence as he leaves the room and locks the door. I put my head in my hands. I have so many questions and I need to know where Marvin is. I try but I can't remember anything at all about what happened. We were in a taxi going to a bar, holding hands, and laughing and then everything goes blank. How is that possible? I eat the food; I'm starving and it's what Marvin would tell me to do. I spy a commode chair in the corner and am relieved that so far this kidnapping seems rather more civilised than the ones I see on the TV. I get up to walk around but think better of it and sit back down. They've obviously got the wrong person. I've no idea where my husband is, or even if he's alive, and if I try and ask any questions or make any moves to get out of here they are going to kill me.

I drift in and out of sleep, shocked every time I wake to realise I am still here. I don't know how long it has been when I hear the door again. I have a plan, not questions, just information. I start my carefully rehearsed speech and surprisingly he lets me speak.

"My name is Marcus. I was in a taxi with my husband, Marvin. I don't remember anything, and I don't know where he is or even if he is alive. I'm scared and I'm going to do everything you say, and I won't try and escape or do anything stupid. I have no idea what has happened or why I'm here. I'm just a chef."

I look him in the eye. I've seen evil, emotionless eyes before but there is humanity there and he didn't flinch when I mentioned either of our names. He puts down another bag of food, another man comes in behind him and I know I've pushed it too far. He is marching towards me and I know I'm done for. I close my eyes and prepare myself, but he walks straight past me and wheels the commode out of the room. It's just the two of us again. I look into his eyes, pleading, hoping that he'll give me something, that he'll take pity on me or realise I'm not the man he's looking for, but he doesn't look at me.

"Halfway there, another twenty-four hours, same rules apply. No questions and no heroics, just follow the rules, trust me."

He looks uncomfortable and I can sense remorse or guilt from him. I can tell he wants to say something else. I feel pathetic but I do exactly as he instructs. I believe him wholeheartedly that I am being watched and that they will kill me if I make a move. I feel guilty about trying to save myself, but what use am I to Marvin if I get myself killed? He is the only thing on my mind. I'm so scared of what might be happening to him. What could anyone want with us? We own a little restaurant and haven't done anything to anyone.

I wake from a sleep I hadn't realised I was in and my captor is in the doorway. I don't speak. There are two men behind him and they have a hood and a gun. After all this they are going to kill me anyway. The hood is shoved over my head, and I feel someone grab my arm and the side of my head.

"Walk with me, and don't try anything stupid. There is a gun pressed against your skull. You take one step out of line and we will shoot."

My legs are disobedient, and I'm scared I'll stumble.

"OK, I will, I promise, don't shoot me." We walk slowly through the door and, after a couple of minutes, I'm aware I am outside.

"You are going home now." I feel a sharp pain explode in my head. I didn't get to say goodbye.

I wake up and open my eyes. I'm lying on the floor and I can feel the hood over my eyes. How did I end up back here again? My head is thumping, and I feel sick. I sit up tentatively and take off the hood, then look around the familiar room. Even in the dark I recognise everything. I am wobbly and lightheaded, but I pull myself to my feet, holding onto my kitchen counter for balance. I'm home.

I lay my head on the cool, hard counter and allow myself to cry for the first time. I cry hard; it's a release. I hadn't dared to even believe it was happening before. I would have crumbled. In the end it was true, I did what they said, and they let me go. But where's Marvin? Did they even take him? I try to run to the stairs, fall and crack my knee and cry out, then scramble to my feet.

"Marvin?" There's no answer. I'm scared, and my voice is shrill and frightened.

"Marvin!" Still no answer. There is a note at the foot of the stairs, sitting on a suitcase, my suitcase.

"Dear Marcus, if you are reading this, they let you go and hopefully that means we are both now safe. I've made a huge mess of everything and I can't begin to tell you how sorry I am. I can't believe I ruined our wonderful life. I got in over my head and I had to use the restaurant to try and save us, but I failed. I had Emil keep you safe until they stopped looking for you. He had to make it look real. I'm so sorry. Take the suitcase and the plane tickets inside and get on the plane. If I am alive, I will meet you there. If not, stay there for a month and call the police before you return. If you don't want me anymore, I understand, I've risked your safety and I will never forgive myself.

Always,

Marvin."

My nice, quiet suburban life has somehow become something out of a bad gangster movie. I sit on the floor and stare at the letter. This can't be happening. What if Marvin is dead? I should destroy the letter, but it might be all I have left of him.

I try to focus and clean myself up. The longer I'm here, the more danger I'm in. The taxi ride to the airport is a blur. My mind is swimming with all this new information, the uninvited and unwelcome changes to my life, and I'm torn between hate and love. I feel he's ruined my life, but he is the most important thing in my life. If I made a mistake, I'd expect his support, but this is more than a mistake - it's a betrayal. I am certain my terror and guilt is written all over my face as I pass seamlessly through security and board the plane. I was expecting Mexico, given the current situation, but the south of France is good. I think I'll be safe.

I step off the plane, with no idea of what awaits me. Will Marvin be here? If he isn't, I don't know what I'm going to do. My heart leaps into my throat as I see a man holding a sign with my name on it. He looks scary, which is good if he's on my side. I can't see any other options.

"Bonjour, je m'appelle Marcus."

"Come with me." He has a strong French accent and grabs my arm, but I instinctively pull it back. I can't risk being taken away again.

"Who are you?"

"Just do as you are told. That worked out last time, non?" He's right, but I'm terrified of being held captive again, even if it is for my own benefit. I let him escort me to the car; it's huge with blacked out windows.

"I'm not..."

"Get in!"

I'm scared of what will happen if I don't, and I'm scared of what will happen if I do. I climb in the back seat and Marvin is there. I am furious but ecstatic; I feel such overwhelming love and relief, but I want to scream. His face is badly bruised and he has a cast on his arm. We cry and we hug and slowly the anger ebbs away.

"I couldn't wait, Marcus. I cannot begin to tell you how sorry I am about everything. I'm so sorry I scared you but all I wanted was you to be safe."

"I was scared, but not now. I'm never scared when I'm with you. Please don't ever leave me alone again like that."

"I won't. I love you."

Even though I know in reality we are far from safe, everything suddenly feels good again. Whatever comes, I know we can take it on together.

Day 28

Once in a Lifetime

I don't know what he's doing here. He looks like a millionaire and nothing on the menu here is more than a tenner. He's avoiding touching anything and hasn't taken a sip of the espresso he ordered. I'll put him out of his misery.

"Would you like the bill, sir? I can take that for you." I gesture to the cup.

He looks at my name tag. "How very observant and thoughtful of you, Felicity."

My nametag says Fliss. No one has called me Felicity since I was a kid. He can't be more than thirty-five, but he speaks as though he were more than twice that.

"No problem. Don't tell them I said so, but everything here is pretty gross."

His laugh is as posh as his voice. "You are beastly, Felicity."

That is easily the oddest thing anyone has ever said to me at work but, looking back, it's certainly one of the more normal things Monty ever said.

He pays in cash and, tucked under the very generous twenty-pound tip, is a note.

"Dear Felicity, I have a job proposition for you. Please call me at your earliest convenience, Montague." His number is written underneath. I stuff it into my pocket, even though it would be crazy to call a random eccentric stranger. Yes, crazy.

After a couple of glasses of wine, with only my cat for company, calling seems like a rather reasonable suggestion, and he answers immediately.

"Good evening."

Who answers the phone like that? "Hi, it's Fliss, I mean Felicity. You asked me to call?"

"Good evening, dear girl, yes. How are we?"

"Good, I think. What..."

"I hate the telephone, so incredibly impersonal. Will you meet me for lunch tomorrow, midday at the Grace Garden hotel? Do you know it?"

"Yes, but..."

"I know you are free; I won't be offended if you just say no."

I can't decide if he's efficient or rude, but I'm intrigued either way, and he's right, I have nothing to do tomorrow. "Yes, I'll be there."

"Good, don't be late. I'll be ordering champagne and oysters."

He hangs up the phone and I decide to have an early night. Tomorrow could be interesting.

I wasn't always a waitress. I know how to dress and behave for lunch at the Grace Garden. He clearly knows how to dress, too, and he looks much less awkward than yesterday, almost handsome. Champagne is on the table and oysters are placed on the table the second I sit down. I love oysters and they look incredible.

"I'm afraid I only have a short time, Felicity, something has come up. I'm dreadfully sorry."

"That's OK, don't worry." We clink glasses and the champagne tastes like heaven.

He hands me a thin brown envelope across the table.

"This includes all the details of my job proposition. Please take it home and read it carefully. It's a one-of-a-kind opportunity but it is not for everyone, so you must read and make sure you understand every single detail."

"Sure, no problem."

He is intense and stiff suddenly. "No, please understand. Initially the offer will look too good to be true, and in some ways it is, but if you are not afraid, then you don't understand."

Clearly, any sensible person would have thanked him and left at this point, but I didn't. I would give anything to go back there.

I'm fuzzy-headed from the champagne so I take a nap before reading the contents of the envelope, despite my curiosity. I read his proposal and I understand it fully. Again, I wasn't always a waitress. I read it once more just to be sure. He is right, I am afraid, but I know instantly that I'm going to accept. I've nothing to lose and everything to gain. There is a written note attached to the front page of the contract.

"You will have everything you desire, money and possessions beyond your wildest dreams. You aren't the first and others have paid dearly for their choice. They all soften eventually, as will you.

Please understand this before you sign,

Monty"

No point putting this off.

"Good evening." His voice is playful, almost mocking.

"Good evening, Monty. I've read everything, and I understand. I am afraid but I want to go ahead."

"Tell me."

"Tell you what?"

"Tell me what you understand." He sounds hard and I am momentarily afraid.

"You will give me a house, a car, all the possessions I could need and a one hundred thousand pound a year salary to be your assistant."

"Good, go on."

"My only job is to bring you someone of your choosing to your house once a month. I don't ask any questions and, if I am ever asked, I was with you."

"Yes. Don't you..."

"I know what you're going to ask, and no, the answer is definitely no. I do not want to know why. I only want the things you are offering me." My mouth is dry and I can't quite believe what I am saying.

He sounds pleased and not surprised. "Very well, Felicity. Bring the signed forms immediately to my office. You will move into your new home on Monday. I will send you the address. Our first outing will be Friday."

"Ok... That's... Yes, OK."

"Once you sign, Felicity, you are bound by the terms of the contract. If you choose not to, then you are free to carry on with the existence you have. You won't hear from me again unless you try to tell anyone of our dealings. Think carefully, Felicity, your predecessor paid with her life."

The line goes dead, but I am weirdly calm. I want what he is offering, and I am willing to pay the price. I'm not doing anything bad to anyone, and if I don't accept it, he'll find someone else. I deserve some luxury and some happiness; it's been way too long.

Moving in is easy. I have little to bring with me and a huge space to put it into. There is a twenty thousand pound "moving in allowance" that comes with the house and I devote the next three days to spending it. All of it.

I am ready on time and dressed as instructed on Friday morning. Monty collects me in the most beautiful vintage sports car. This is the life.

"Listen carefully, Felicity, the instructions for today are especially important. I appreciate this is your first assignment, but if you don't do exactly as I ask, it will be your last. Do we understand each other?"

Assignment? I suddenly feel like a secret agent. "Yes, of course."

He smiles a kind smile but his eyes tell a different story. "For today, you are my business manager. You will be meeting Matilda at the Grace Garden. She is a potential candidate for my PA, and you will be checking her documents before escorting her to my house for her final interview. Check the documents only, and do not ask her any personal questions. I would like her at the house at 1pm exactly. George will pick you both up. When you drop her off, you are to leave immediately. George will take you home. I will call you in exactly one week and you will not leave your house until then. Understand?"

"Yes, but one week? I don't have..."

"You do, it's all taken care of. Do you understand?"

"Yes. Yes, I do."

I understand exactly and I avoid letting out any of the questions that are rushing through my mind. They are not helpful and will only ruin this for me.

"Perfect, shall we have some music? Do you like jazz?"

Matilda is not what I was expecting. She is non-descript, completely forgettable. I do as he says and check her documents. She tries to engage with me, and I suspect she thinks it will help her get the job. I am cold and business-like. I never meet her eyes, not once. The transaction is seamless and, as I watch her walk into the house with Monty, I feel very little. I've learned over the years to disconnect. It's what you need to survive.

A month passes, I ignore the news, it's not my problem. I stay away from everyone. I have everything I need now, and they'll only spoil it for me. Over the next two months, I interview two more potential Personal Assistants at the Grace Garden. They both go as smoothly as the first, and

I do exactly as I am told. I don't sleep as well as I used to. I made a stupid mistake one night and read too much, and now I know their full names, I know there are people looking for them. What keeps me going though, is that I honestly don't know where they are. Maybe they've been given top secret job opportunities in Monty's firm. I won't be able to kid myself forever. I'm starting to feel the weight of the bodies on my shoulders.

Today is number four. Monty collects me, and I feel robotic.

"Felicity, good heavens. That suit is hanging off you. The waif look does suit you, but do be sure to buy a new wardrobe."

He is very upbeat today. I muster a smile and a nod behind my dark glasses.

"Are you weakening, Felicity? It's a little early but I need you to be honest if you are."

"No, I'm fine. A little early?"

"I usually get six or maybe eight before the heaviness sets in. Do you feel the heaviness, Felicity?"

I do. He has described it perfectly. I feel weighed down, squashed, like I won't be able to breath or move soon. "No, I'm sorry. I'm just not myself today."

He is irritated. "Well, become yourself by the end of this car ride. We have a deal and I'd hate for you to ruin it for yourself."

I want to cry.

I hate the Grace Garden now. What once seemed beautiful is now pretentious and ugly, but I know what I have to do.

"Hi, Jodi, lovely to meet you. Did you bring everything I asked?"

She nods and hands me an envelope. I feel a sharp pain in my chest, and I drop the envelope onto the floor. I know her. No, that's not true, I don't know her, but I've seen her. In the park. Pushing a buggy.

"Are you OK?" She looks kind and genuinely concerned.

"Yes. Yes, I'm so very sorry. I just felt lightheaded all of a sudden."

I busy myself with the envelope and try to stop my chest heaving with panic.

"I'm sorry, there isn't a copy of your driving licence here, Jodi. I can't take you to interview. Could you go home and get it please?"

"I'm so sorry, I wasn't asked to bring that. Yes, of course. Should I come back..."

I answer too quickly and loudly, "No! I mean, no, don't worry, I'll call you in an hour and arrange your interview. Please don't worry, it's not your fault."

I'm not keeping things in anymore. They are spilling out of the sides for the world to see. "George, take me to Monty. She didn't have everything."

"Felicity, they all try this. You'll end up just like them."

"George, just take me to Monty. She's gone home to get what she needs."

He sighs and I know he's seen this all before, but not with me. I can make it different. I can make him see sense. In any case, I can't take anyone else to him and I'll have to accept what is coming.

He doesn't seem surprised to see me alone at the door. He raises an eyebrow.

"Monty, she has a child!"

He seems bored and exasperated. "I told you, we don't ask anything personal."

"I didn't. I recognised her. It doesn't matter anyway, I've sent her away. Pick someone else."

He laughs mockingly and I can feel the anger. "So Felicity, people without children are disposable, are they?"

"That's not..."

"The other three didn't matter because they hadn't spawned? Or at least you assumed they hadn't."

"Did they..."

"That's not important anymore, is it? Listen very carefully, Felicity. I am happy to pick someone else, just this once. But then you're done. We are done."

Maybe this will all work out after all. I know I've been at least partially involved in something terrible, but if I get out now, maybe things can go back to the way they were.

"I choose you, Felicity."

"What?"

"It's either you or her, you decide. I really don't care, either way I know I'm going to have lots of fun."

I have nothing to say.

"Be back here in exactly an hour. Bring her back or bring yourself."

He closes the door and I run past George. I run and I run until my legs turn to jelly, I run until I think I can't run anymore, and then I keep running. I know what I have to do. There is no good way out of this now but I have to salvage what I can. I make it to the door, my chest heaving and my face stained with tears.

"How can I help you?" I'm not at all sure anyone can help me, but I need to try.

"Officer, I need to report a very serious crime. Can I talk to someone in private?"

He writes down my name and takes the piece of paper to another police officer who looks like he may be in charge. I know I am in serious trouble, but at least this way Jodi and I will stay alive.

"Would you come with me please?" He escorts me to an interview room and hands me a much-needed cup of tea.

"You'll be safe here. Someone will be with you shortly."

He leaves and I feel relaxed, exhausted even. It's been a long time coming, but I'm doing the right thing and, if I help them, who knows, maybe I won't spend the rest of my life behind bars. I put my head on the table and try to keep my eyes open but within minutes I am sound asleep.

I am woken by a familiar voice. His face is inches from mine and his lips are pulled back over his teeth as he speaks.

"Tut tut, Felicity, you really are beastly, aren't you?"

I see the syringe in his hand, but it's too late, it's already in my neck.

The End!

You've finished!

Well done for persevering and completing the full 28 days. It's an amazing achievement and shows commitment to your own wellbeing. I hope you've learned that it's perfectly OK and achievable to spend a small amount of time each day doing something that is just for you.

Have a think about which of the stories you liked (or which you didn't) and pick a book you would like to read. There are millions of amazing novels out there to suit every possible taste. Start as soon as you can, tomorrow if possible. Keep your habit up and your expectations low. If you can read for fifteen minutes every day, then you'll read many wonderful books in your lifetime.

Thank you for taking this journey with me, and I wish you years of happiness and wonderful stories.

Printed in Great Britain
by Amazon

78730482R00068